www.MinotaurBooks.com

**The premier website
for the best in crime fiction.**

Log on and learn more about:

The Labyrinth: Sign up for this monthly newsletter and get your crime fiction fix. Commentary, author Q&A, hot new titles, and giveaways.

MomentsInCrime: It's no mystery what our authors are thinking. Each week, a new author blogs about their upcoming projects, special events, and more. Log on today to talk to your favorite authors.
www.MomentsInCrime.com

GetCozy: The ultimate cozy connection. Find your favorite cozy mystery, grab a reading group guide, sign up for monthly giveaways, and more.
www.GetCozyOnline.com

"Hess fans will find much to entertain them."
        —Publishers Weekly on *Damsels in Distress*

"Lively, sharp, irreverent."
        —The New York Times Book Review on *Poisoned Pins*

"Larcenous shenanigans…breezy throughout."
        —Chicago Tribune on *Poisoned Pins*

"With her wry asides, Claire makes a most engaging narrator. The author deftly juggles the various plot strands…the surprising denouement comes off with éclat."   *—Publishers Weekly* on *Out on a Limb*

"A winning blend of soft-core feminism, trendy sub-plots, and a completely irreverent style that character-izes both the series and the sleuth."
        —Houston Chronicle

"A wildly entertaining series."   *—Mystery Scene*

"Joan Hess is one of the best mystery writers in the world. She makes it look so easy that few readers and fewer critics realize what a rare talent hers is."
        —Elizabeth Peters, author of *Tomb of the Golden Bird*

"Joan Hess is seriously funny. Moreover, she is seri-ously kind as well as clever when depicting the follies, foibles, and fantasies of our lives. Viva Joan!"
        —Carolyn Hart, author of *Dead Days of Summer*

"Fresh and funny…her trademark humor is stamped on every page."
        —Publishers Weekly on *The Goodbye Body*

TICKLED
TO DEATH

A CLAIRE MALLOY MYSTERY

Joan Hess

St. Martin's Paperbacks

This is a work of fiction. All of the characters, organizations and events portrayed in this novel are either products of the author's imagination or are used fictitiously.

TICKLED TO DEATH

Copyright © 1994 by Joan Hess.

For information address St. Martin's Press, 175 Fifth Avenue, New York, NY 10010.

EAN: 978-0-312-38464-7

Printed in the United States of America

Dutton edition published 1994
Onyx edition / May 1995
St. Martin's Paperbacks edition / November 2010

St. Martin's Paperbacks are published by St. Martin's Press, 175 Fifth Avenue, New York, NY 10010.

10 9 8 7 6 5 4 3 2 1

For Mackie and Bob Cutting,

with love and admiration

1

"No," Luanne said after a goodly amount of thought, "I don't suppose he's the perfect potential mate. There's a possibility he murdered his wife."

"I suppose that could be considered a flaw," I said as I stared across the picnic table at a woman who heretofore had seemed a singular beacon of sanity in a world beset with neon. We were sitting in the beer garden on a balmy June evening for the first time in several weeks. We usually met every Wednesday, but I'd been badgered night and day by my spotty old accountant, who reputedly glows in the dark during tax season, and for most of a month I'd been hiding out in either the back of my bookstore or my bathtub (sessions in the former dictate sessions in the latter). I finally found my voice and said, "Exactly how strong is this possibility?"

"The whole thing's absurd, but the investigator from the sheriff's office continues to pester

Dick several times a week. The poor baby—and I don't mean this captain, who's an anal-retentive jerk—is getting an ulcer, and his performance in the sack is indicative of his stress. Were I a saint, I wouldn't even notice, but it's become a factor."

I was perplexed by Luanne's attitude. She'd survived a divorce and a migration from a wealthy Connecticut suburb to distinctly middle-class Farberville, an amiable town of several thousand college students and twenty-odd thousand civilians. She presumably made enough money from her funky used-clothing store, Secondhand Rose, to keep herself in beer and pretzels. Her hair was dramatic—black with streaks of silver. Her Yankee-boarding-school accent was rarely discernible. And she was in the midst of an affair with a man who might have murdered his wife.

I replenished my cup from the pitcher, then said, "You're quite sure he didn't?"

"Dick wouldn't step on a spider. He's a pedodontist, and he spends his days putting braces on little teeth for great big fees. He donates time to a community clinic, attends the Episcopal church on major holidays, and calls his mother every Sunday night. He's a decent golfer and an avid racquetball player. He makes his own pesto. He can sew a button on a shirt. Does this sound like the résumé of a murderer?"

"Then why does the investigator keep implying that he is?" I asked with impressive reasonableness. "Surely there must be some sort of case."

"Becca died in a boating accident, but Captain Gannet is determined to prove Dick masterminded it."

"A boating accident?"

Luanne automatically reached for a pack of cigarettes that was not there, sighed, and began to shred a napkin. "Dick has a gorgeous house at Turnstone Lake that he and Becca used every weekend. There's a private bird sanctuary in the area. It consists of a few thousand acres of abandoned pastures, forests, and swampy creeks, and it supports a large population of bald-headed eagles in the winter. Eagles are an endangered species, you know, as are hawks, owls, and even turkey buzzards. It's a federal offense to so much as muss their feathered heads."

"This is all terribly interesting," I said, yawning. "Shall we move on to the accident?"

"Becca received a phone call late one afternoon that an eagle was flapping about on one of the islands, so she went down to the marina to take their boat out to investigate. Halfway to the island, there was an explosion, probably caused by a propane leak in the cabin."

I gave her a Miss Marplish smile. "How do we know she received a call?"

"She left a message on Agatha Anne Gallinago's answering machine. Agatha Anne's the president of the foundation that owns the sanctuary. As soon as she arrived home and found the message, she drove to the marina to try to catch Becca before she took the boat. She and the manager at the marina both saw the explosion."

"And this purported leak?" I continued delicately. "Why not sabotage of some sort?"

"Agatha Anne smelled gas earlier that day and reported it to the manager, who admitted he hadn't done anything about it. It didn't occur to either of them that anyone would use the boat."

"If it's all so straightforward, replete with witnesses and odoriferous leakage, why is this captain suspicious of your pesto-making prince? Law enforcement agencies don't have the manpower to hound innocent citizens to any great extent. There must be some reason that you haven't mentioned."

Luanne shrugged. "Well, the night before the accident, Dick and Becca had an argument at one of the bird group's parties. She threw a piece of quiche at him, so he stormed out of the house and walked home." She was trying to sound nonchalant, but her eyes flickered nervously and the pile of white shreds was growing steadily. If she'd not quit smoking, I was quite sure she would have had a cigarette in each hand and another smoldering in an ashtray. "He was so angry that he drove back to town and didn't return until the next night. A deputy arrived shortly afterward to tell him the news."

"When did all this take place?"

"About three months ago," she said in a low

mumble, no doubt hoping the chatter from the adjoining tables would drown out her words.

As the mother of a teenager, I was accustomed to such evasive tactics and adept at exposing them. "Did you meet him at the funeral, Luanne, or were you lurking behind a headstone in the cemetery?"

"I met him two weeks ago at the bank. We chatted, then ended up having coffee. One thing led to another. I really thought I'd found the perfect man. Dick's good-looking, rich, sensitive, virile . . . and available. He took me to his lake house last weekend. It's not especially large, but it's equipped with every appliance in the western world, and has an enormous redwood deck. I can already imagine myself in a lacy little something, gazing at the sunset while Dick nibbles my neck and murmurs about our prenuptial contract. When he actually proposes, I shall be in the conservatory, dressed in a white frock and holding a red rose. The challenge is to find a conservatory which isn't crowded by the likes of Professor Plum and Miss Scarlet and their lead pipes and candlesticks."

The arithmetic was not challenging, especially to someone with a meticulous accountant like mine. "We'll worry about the conservatory when the time comes. Perfect men do not leap into an affair ten weeks after becoming widowers. The corpse may be cold by now, granted, but has he had time to clean out her closet and throw away her toothbrush?"

"I didn't examine the toothbrushes," Luanne said with only the tiniest glint of guilt. "There are a few things in her closet, such as an Imelda Marcos shoe collection, three fur coats, and enough clothes for an entire sorority house. The woman did like to shop."

I spotted youths with frizzy ponytails unloading instruments and amplifiers by the back gate. "I think you're out of your mind to get involved with this man, and I'll say as much in the eulogy. I need to relieve Caron at the store so that she and Inez can terrorize the mall." I finished the last swallow of beer and stood up, trying to disguise my annoyance. Luanne Bradshaw was in her mid-forties and more than old enough to date whomever she chose. If nothing else, he'd persuaded her to stop smoking. I could only hope he wouldn't persuade her to stop breathing.

She picked up her purse and we pushed our way through the throng and out to the sidewalk. Across the street, none of the pedestrians were streaming into the Book Depot, my source of income and ulcers, but that was hardly surprising. The little man who'd sold it to me had warned me not to anticipate wealth within the millennium, but I was burdened with a daughter to support. At least once a week I was reminded that I was not doing so in a style she found acceptable.

"The captain may be hounding Dick because of his first wife's death," Luanne said as we seized a break in the traffic and stepped off the curb.

I froze in the middle of the street. "And there's a possibility that he murdered her, too? Luanne, you're safer standing here than allowing your neck to be nibbled by this pedodontist. You're hardly practicing safe sex if you're sleeping with Bluebeard."

"I think not," she said, shoving me into motion as a convertible filled with hooting fraternity boys bore down on us. "He didn't murder her, either. The only problem is that her death wasn't explained to Captain Gannet's satisfaction. As I said, he's anal-retentive."

"You'd better pray he's not right."

We stopped under the portico that had once protected passengers as they awaited trains that would carry them to exotic places like New Orleans and Omaha. These days they'd have a futile wait, but they could entertain themselves looking at my very dusty window display of histories and mysteries.

I made a note to utilize the feather duster on a more regular basis, then said, "I am not your mother, and it's none of my business if you want to have a meaningful relationship with a homicidal maniac."

"He's a wonderful man," she said, her voice thickening and her eyes filling with tears. "None of this is his fault. When Carlton was killed, nobody came pounding on your doors with accusations and innuendoes."

"Carlton died in a head-on collision with a chicken truck," I retorted, "and the culpable driver was standing there in a flurry of white feathers when the state police arrived. It's hardly the same situation—and it happened once, not twice. Or who knows how many times, to be brutally frank. This man could have buried a bevy of grade-school sweethearts and fiancées along the way."

Luanne opened her mouth, then clamped it shut and stalked away without acknowledging the perspicacity of my remarks. I went inside, where Caron and Inez were entertaining each other by reading aloud from *Lady Chatterley's Lover.* Reminding myself the novel was a literary classic, if not precisely penned in hopes of sending fifteen-year-olds into paroxysms of snickers, I went behind the counter to make sure the contents of the cash register were not seriously depleted.

"Flowers in her public hair? That's gross!" shrieked Caron, who inherited my curly red hair and freckles but not one hint of my mild-mannered personality. She staggered out of sight behind the fiction rack, hiccuping with glee, and returned with a gardening book. "Pansies of passion? Dahlias of desire? Lilies of lust?"

As far as I can determine, Caron's every act is

dictated by hormones. These last few years have been a series of Broadway theater productions, but I can never tell if we're to be drawn into a dark and brooding drama or a musical comedy. Or, more frequently, an off-Broadway experimental piece that mystifies the cast as much as the audience. She has long since mastered the art of speaking in capital letters, and her lower lip sticks out most of the time to indicate her displeasure with someone who has patience, maternal acumen, and stretch marks.

Inez Thornton is quite the opposite. She is limp and anemic but ever loyal. Her thick lenses disguise her occasional winces when Caron's volume rises to an unseemly level, and she keeps a judicious eye on the nearest exit. She is still in the throes of lowercase, and at the moment she was turning pink. "Hello, Mrs. Malloy," she said as if my presence would have any damper on Caron's behavior.

"Snapdragons of salaciousness!" Caron shrieked before once again disappearing.

"Aren't you two going to the mall?" I said optimistically. "Everything's on sale, and you don't want to miss a minute."

"Zinnias of zest!"

If there'd been any customers, I might have felt obliged to put a stop to this litany of floral lasciviousness, but I was curious to learn the extent of Caron's vocabulary in such matters.

"Everlastings of eroticism!"

Inez had edged in front of the self-help books and was regarding me with the wide-eyed solemnity of a seal pup. "Actually, we're not going to the mall after all. Rhonda Maguire got her driver's license this morning and she's picking up everybody for pizza."

"Dandelions of depression," came a groan.

"Afterward, some of the football players are coming to Rhonda's to swim," Inez added. "Louis Wilderberry called her this afternoon."

"Wilderberries of wantonness . . ."

Inez frowned at this latest contribution. "I don't think there are plants called wilderberries, Caron. His name is an anglicized version of whatever it was in German or Polish or something like that. His sister told me that at band practice."

Caron came around the rack. "Are you implying that I am botanically impaired? I know Perfectly Well that his name is German or whatever. I was attempting to make a point, not pass a course."

I shooed them away, locked the store, and walked back to our apartment, the second story of a white brick house across the street from the verdant lawn of Farber College. The Kappa Theta Eta house next to us was boarded up, and no longer were we treated to sisterly squeals at all hours of the night. I'd solved a murder for them, but apparently they'd not resolved their ensuing problems with the home office (aka National). I had not mourned the loss of a group that dressed in pink, coddled cats, and drank Tab and bourbon.

Peter Rosen arrived within the hour, looking less than dapper in a rumpled suit and unbuttoned collar. He has black hair, a jutting nose, and deceptively gentle brown eyes that have been known to narrow into unattractive slits when he's perturbed. Lately, our relationship had become as tempestuous as my daughter on a bad day. I wasn't sure if the source of tension lay in his muted but never absent arrogance or my unwillingness to make a commitment that would result in a division of closet space.

We also had intermittent confrontations when I went out of my way to assist the police when they were being bullheaded and blind. Peter, when caught up in his position as a lieutenant in the Farberville Criminal Investigation Department, takes exception to my invaluable contributions to truth and justice. He's been known to accuse me of meddling and threaten me with incarceration. Once he'd had my car impounded out of what I felt was nothing more than spite. Such things are not conducive to a harmonious relationship.

He accepted my offer of a beer, begged quite charmingly for a sandwich, and sank down on the couch. I provided him with said sustenance and then sat down at a marginally civil distance.

"My mother," he said with melancholy, "has

decided she wants to spend at least a week of her final days on a cruise ship. If I allow her to go alone, they may well be her final days. She'll fall off the end of the ship within hours. I'll be stricken with remorse for the rest of my life."

"So go with her."

"I don't want to go with her. She'll pick up some pudgy condo salesman in the bar the first night, and then parade around with him as if they were the Duke and Duchess of Windsor."

"I thought you said she was going to fall overboard, not in love."

"Maybe it's one and the same," he said, no doubt thinking himself quite the cryptic. He gave me the opportunity to ask what he meant, but I looked incuriously at him and then at my watch. "I don't suppose you want to come along and help me chaperon my white-haired seductress?" he added. "She has enough money to buy the ship. Surely she'll spring for a ticket so that her beloved son won't sulk in the bar while she plays roulette with her boyfriend."

"You suppose correctly. I've developed claustrophobia in my old age."

"Are you talking about a cruise ship or a relationship?"

"I'm too tired for profundities," I said as I finished my drink and again looked at my watch. "You'd better run along and call a travel agent. Your mother's getting older by the minute."

To what I suspected was mutual relief, he gave

me a passionless kiss on the cheek and left. It was possible I was as crazy as Luanne, I thought as I tidied up the living room. I'd just turned down a Caribbean cruise with a man who had never been suspected of murdering an ex-wife, having opted for a routine divorce. He met all of Luanne's criteria: good-looking, rich, sensitive, virile . . . and available. I doubted he could sew on a button or whip up a batch of pesto, but stress had never affected his performance in the sack. Peter was a man of many talents; regrettably, his most pronounced one these days was his ability to irritate me.

I heard from no one of any interest over the next few days, and on Saturday morning I was diligently dusting the window display (and sneezing explosively) when the telephone rang. My accountant had mentioned my second quarterly payment only the week before, and I was leery as I picked up the receiver.

Luanne bypassed the customary pleasantries. "Claire, I need your help! The most terrible thing has happened, and there's no one else I can turn to. I couldn't stop pacing last night, much less get any sleep, and now I—"

"What's wrong?" I asked in the voice that slows Caron down when she's describing Rhonda Maguire's latest incursion into perfidy.

"Captain Gannet came to the house at midnight and took Dick away for questioning. I called this morning, but all I got was a runaround from a simpering idiot who can't be old enough to shave, much less be issued a weapon. He told me not to bother to go to the office because they won't let me see Dick. If I knew the name of Dick's lawyer, I could at least call him. Should I hunt through his drawers for an address book?"

"Dick can call his lawyer himself." I paused to sort through her babbled words. "He was taken away for questioning, you said? He wasn't arrested?"

"What difference does it make?" she wailed.

"It makes a big difference, Luanne. Have they found new evidence to link him to his wife's"—I made myself use the word least likely to send her into more wails of desperation—"accident?"

"Gannet didn't say. He just showed up at the door, ordered Dick to get dressed, and then put him in the car and drove away. Dick has a rifle in the closet. I'm going to drive over there and demand that they let me speak to Dick."

"No!" I gripped the receiver and frantically tried to think how to deter my best friend from being gunned down in the doorway of the sheriff's office. "Under no circumstances are you to so much as open the closet door. Give me directions to the house. I'll leave here as soon as I can track down Caron so she can mind the store."

She gushed with gratitude, then rattled off highway numbers, county road numbers, turns onto roads that lacked numbers, and an admonishment to watch for deer during the last few miles. I reiterated my promise, hung up, and called Caron at Inez's house.

"I have plans," she said, unmoved by my plea. "It was whispered last night that my body is the precise color of bread, which certain people found hilarious. The sun is shining. I intend to lie out and finish that book about pubic hair. I shall resemble toast by the end of the afternoon, and Rhonda can just take her tacky—"

"You'll have to do it tomorrow," I said, equally unmoved. "Luanne needs my help, and I cannot close the store on a Saturday. If you want to keep yourself in suntan oil, you'd better get over here in the next fifteen minutes."

Caron's compassion runs no deeper than her epidermis, but she is aware of the relationship between business activity and her own well-developed materialism. She and Inez arrived half an hour later. I gave one the feather duster and the other a lecture about not reading aloud from anything racier than Dr. Seuss, grabbed my scrawled directions, and left for Turnstone Lake, which was about forty miles from Farberville.

I followed the numbers easily, but once I left the pavement for a series of dirt roads, I became confused. Luanne had mentioned signs nailed on a post. There was no post. If I'd passed another car, or an inhabited dwelling, I could have asked directions, but as it was, I felt as though I'd abandoned society for some sort of primeval immersion. The sloping woods were dappled with sunlight. Orange hawkweed bloomed in the shadowy retreats, and black-eyed Susans lined the ditches. A hawk circled high above a hilltop.

I might have enjoyed this incursion into nature, but I was keenly aware that I couldn't even find the lake. I wadded up the paper with the directions and tossed it into the backseat, gritted my teeth, and started turning left or right at each opportunity. My hatchback shuddered as I careened down and up the increasingly bad roads until I was on nothing better than a logging trail. The only water I'd encountered was a mushy puddle that left blinding brown splashes on the hood and windshield. I, a renowned amateur sleuth who'd utilized the smallest of clues to expose heinous crimes and unspeakable treachery (or an abundance of greed, anyway), was incapable of finding a large lake. Had my ego been less fragile, I might have found the experience humbling.

I ran the wipers until I could see between the streaks, then took off once more. Several turns later I spotted a stout woman dressed in a wrinkled skirt, a baggy sweatshirt, heavy leather shoes, and a molded plastic pith helmet. As I stopped next to her, she turned and lowered a pair of binoculars.

"Good morning," she said, giving me a vaguely startled smile. "I'm on the trail of a hairy woodpecker. He is a shy fellow, and difficult to spot. I heard him only minutes ago, unless, of course, I mistook his hammering for that of his cousin, the downy woodpecker." She cupped a hand around her ear and listened intently. "I don't hear him now."

"I'm sorry if I alarmed him," I said meekly.

"Ah, well."

"I'm lost. I've been driving around these roads for half an hour. Can you aim me in the direction of the lake?"

"The lake covers thirty thousand acres, my dear. We're on what is basically a peninsula, with water on three sides of us."

I hunted around in the backseat until I found my discarded directions. "I'm looking specifically for Dick Cissel's house on Blackburn Creek."

"Oh, you have strayed, haven't you? It's a good three miles from here. Let me fetch my bag and I'll ride there with you. My hairy woodpecker is much too shy to show himself anymore today." She took an enormous handbag from a branch and awkwardly climbed into my car. "I'm Livia Dunling, and you're a friend of Dick's. We stay on this road until the second turn to the right."

"I'm Claire Malloy. I've never met Dick. A friend of mine is at his house, and she asked me to come."

Livia rummaged through her bag and took out a plastic pillbox and a canteen. After she'd swallowed a pill, she returned the items to the bag. "While I was filling the feeders this morning, I saw your friend on the deck. She appeared very distraught. I considered going to the house to see if I could comfort her, but I began to feel fluttery and went inside to lie down. I have a most aggravating heart problem."

I wasn't sure what confidences I should share with my passenger. "You live near Dick?" I asked cautiously.

"Directly across the cove. My husband and I own Dunling Lodge. I wanted to call it Dun-Roaming, but Wharton does not appreciate whimsy. He'll be most displeased when he learns I've lost the jeep again. I don't suppose you noticed it parked beneath a particularly fine specimen of wild dogwood?"

"No, I'm afraid not."

"That's the driveway," she said as she swung open the car door.

I jammed on the brakes in time to prevent her from tumbling under the tires to a certain death. "Thank you so much, Mrs. Dunling," I said between gasps. "Are you sure I can't take you to your front door?"

"No, no, I shall hike down by the gully where Wharton reported a hooded warbler only yesterday. He was certain he heard the distinctively flirtatious *tawee-tawee-tawee-tee-o*. Have a nice visit with your friend."

She limped across the road and into the woods, her bag thumping arrhythmically against her broad hips, her binoculars held aloft in one hand should they be called into immediate action.

Feeling inordinately guilty about frightening away the hairy woodpecker, I waited until she'd disappeared, then drove down the driveway and parked beside a forest-green Range Rover. The front of the house was an unimposing expanse of native rockwork with only a few high windows. Landscaping consisted of neglected shrubs and a flagstone sidewalk. I had not yet seen the lake, but I heard the drone of a motorboat and deduced its proximity.

The front door opened before I could ring the bell, and Luanne gave me a radiant smile. "Oh good, you're just in time for a Bloody Mary on the deck. Dick is so excited to be meeting you."

2

"What do you mean?" I sputtered, perhaps un-
attractively. "I thought you were planning a
commando raid on the cellblock to rescue this
man. In order to save your life, I came racing
across the county, bouncing down miserable little back roads—"

"They brought him back an hour ago," Luanne
said as she pulled me into a room with a vaulted
ceiling, hand-hewn beams, and a rock fireplace
that soared a good twenty feet and was broad
enough to roast an ox. Even to an untrained eye
like mine, the furnishings were expensive, all natural fibers and muted colors. The wall in front of us
was predominantly glass, and I finally saw the
lake spread out like a sparkling field. Sailboats
bobbled, while motorboats streaked past them
and party barges chugged more sedately. On the
far side were rolling mountains and a few houses
visible among the trees.

"An hour ago?" I said. "That would have

been about the time I arrived at the first of many dead ends. It's a good thing you didn't give the army directions to Kuwait. They'd be floundering around Siberia to this day."

Luanne had the decency to look somewhat abashed. "Don't tell Dick I called you in hysterics, please. I told him I invited you out for lunch."

"We're already telling lies to Mr. Right?" I said as I removed her hand.

"I don't want him to think for an instant that I have any doubts about his innocence. He's trying to be blasé about it, but he snarled at Jillian for using all the hot water, and—"

I may have been a wee bit out of control by now. "Jillian? Is this another applicant for marital murder?"

"Dick didn't murder anyone! He's the one who's being victimized by this investigation." She glanced at a deck strewn with wicker furniture, then hustled me into a bedroom with neatly made twin beds and an aura of staleness that suggested it was a guest room. She sat down on one of the beds and wrapped her arms around herself. To herself as much as to me, she said, "I'm trying so hard to be positive and supportive, to smile and say the right things, to listen with just the right amount of sympathy. Maybe I'm being a hypocrite, but my relationship with Dick is so important that I'd put on an apron and make a casserole if he asked me to."

"You don't know how to put on an apron," I said as I sat across from her. "So who's Jillian?"

"Dick's daughter from his first marriage. She graduated from an Eastern women's college a year ago, and now she mopes around the house, and occasionally answers the telephone and does filing at the foundation office. I'm making every effort to get along with her, but sometimes I want to throttle her. Then I start feeling sorry for her and start thinking about making her a casserole, too!"

My last stirrings of anger evaporated. We'd been friends for several years, and never before had I heard the intensity in her voice when she talked about making a casserole for a man—or anyone else.

"All right," I said, "I'm merely here for a Bloody Mary and lunch, but you have to promise to call me after you get back to Farberville so we can discuss all this. You owe me big, Luanne. This isn't as bad as when you coerced me into assisting you with that ditzy beauty pageant, but I haven't found my way back to the highway yet, either."

We went out to the deck. One of the wicker chairs produced a man with silver hair, bloodshot blue eyes, and darkly tanned skin. He was no taller than Luanne, but beneath a worn cotton sweater, his shoulders were wide and his waist well controlled for his age, which I estimated to be fifty. None of his features was worthy of accolades, but when he smiled at me, I felt bathed in a sensual glow. Luanne was right. He was sexy.

"Dick Cissel," he said as he offered me a hand that had probed crooked teeth in countless little mouths. "I've been looking forward to meeting you. Luanne has told me some pretty interesting stories about you. Shall I fix you a Bloody Mary or would you prefer something else?" He indicated a table crowded with bottles, an ice bucket, glasses, and other essentials.

"I'd love a Bloody Mary," I said as I gave Luanne a dark look. Resisting the urge to mention a few "pretty interesting stories" I'd heard about him, I went to the rail and watched a skier swish out of view. On an adjoining hill was a stone house with three stories of curtainless windows and a veranda edged with flower beds and shrubs. No one was in sight, but birds were attacking the dozen or so feeders with varied degrees of aggression.

"Is that Dunling Lodge?" I asked, calculating the distance. The birds were nothing but dark spots against the sky, and the flowers indistinguishable masses of color. If Livia Dunling had seen Luanne's expression, she'd done so with the aid of her binoculars. I wondered if she had an unimpeded view of the windows in the master bedroom.

Dick brought me a drink. "Yes. Wharton

bought it for Livia as a surprise when he retired from the army. It seems it was a fashionable hotel in its heyday, and he took her there on their honeymoon forty years ago. Twenty years ago it was no longer fashionable, and ultimately it was abandoned. Wharton arranged for all the repairs and remodeling, then put her in the car one afternoon and presented her with it."

"Isn't that romantic?" said Luanne in the breathless voice of a romance-novel heroine. She leaned into Dick, her shoulder rubbing his, her expression as gooey as her voice. I fully expected her to bat her eyelashes and call him Rhett.

"Definitely," I said in the curt voice of someone who'd been dragged across the country for no reason. I was rewarded with an extended tongue, and reciprocated in kind.

Dick either missed or ignored our petty exchange. "It was built back in the thirties as a WPA project, so modernizing the wiring and plumbing must have required a lot of cash. He only remodeled the main floor. The rooms on the top two floors are coated with mildew and filled with junky furniture. There's a bat colony in the attic. Jan and I used to sit out here at sunset and watch them stream out from beneath the eaves."

"Jan was Father's first wife," said a flat voice.

"Why, Jillian," Luanne said, spinning around and edging away from Dick as though she'd realized he was a leper, "I didn't hear you come back. Did you get what you needed at the office?"

Dick motioned to the shadowy figure standing inside the living room. "Come meet a friend of Luanne's and have a drink with us."

The young woman who halted in the doorway was distinctly solid, and apt to be stolid as well. Her brown hair was short and straight, her forehead bisected by bangs, and her nose the only dominant feature on her round face. She wore a beige skirt and blouse and run-down loafers. Ignoring Luanne and me, she said, "No thank you, Father. I have to take a proof page to the print shop in Farberville. I put a pan of frozen lasagna in the oven, and there's a fresh salad in the refrigerator. The rolls are on the counter."

"You didn't have to go to any trouble," Luanne said with a strained but determined smile. "I was going to fix something light."

"I'm in the habit of preparing Father's meals," she said with no smile whatsoever as she disappeared into the living room. Seconds later, a door slammed.

Dick gestured for us to sit down in the oversized wicker chairs. "Jillian didn't mean anything, Luanne. She's just worried about this mess and feels as helpless as I do. Gannet is going to retire at the end of the year, so all we have to do is ride out six more months of his vindictiveness and I'll be a free man. I'll also be certifiably insane, but that's to be expected after marathon sessions with a man with reptilian breath and dandruff."

"Luanne mentioned this Captain Gannet," I

said, disregarding a muffled snort from a nearby chair.

Dick grimaced. "I picked up some gossip about him at that little store by the turnoff. It seems the Gannet family has lived in this area for numerous generations. They were forced to sell their property when the lake was put in, and now the old homestead is under thirty feet of water, as are the bones of the ancestors and Captain Gannet's cherished boyhood haunts. They sold under protest and to this day continue to resent the lake and those of us who can afford weekend houses and boats. Gannet has elected to take out his hostility on me."

"Isn't there something you can do?" Luanne asked, this time sounding as if she might call him Ward and show him the Beaver's report card.

"If I could lure him into my office chair, I'd wire his jaws closed. Then I'd pump him full of Smurf gas and let him giggle to death."

"Smurf gas?" I said blankly.

"Nitrous oxide. One of our patients named it that and the staff adopted it. We're big on stickers and balloons and cute euphemisms."

I had no idea what a Smurf was, but I let it go and returned to a more concrete arena. "Why does Captain Gannet continue to investigate this accident?"

Dick gave Luanne a wry glance, then said, "I should have suspected you'd be curious, Claire. Luanne has told me that you're Farberville's most famous and successful sleuth. I'm not well read in the mystery genre, but I do like the old detective movies. Am I supposed to offer you a retainer? It'll have to be a plastic one with a wire, but they come in all colors these days."

I wasn't sure how genuine his amusement was. I myself was a little disgruntled to discover I'd been the topic of conversation and that he'd been regaled with my past involvements with homicide investigations. Then again, the phrase "most famous and successful" had a measure of charm. "I'm not a private investigator," I said. "There have been a few situations in which the circumstances required me to make a civic-minded contribution."

"You're too modest," murmured Dick.

"Perhaps Luanne exaggerates," I countered evenly.

Luanne stood up, visibly torn between diving over the rail or dashing inside the house. "I'd better check the lasagna. Jillian didn't say how long to leave it in the oven."

He grabbed her hand and pulled her back down. "If Claire wants to investigate the case, she's welcome to do so. Someone has to convince Gannet that it was nothing more than an unfortunate accident."

I put my drink on the table and picked up my purse. "I didn't come here to investigate anything. I don't know what Luanne told you, but I'm not a pushy broad with a twitchy nose and an arsenal in a knitting bag. I think I'd better mind my own business, which is selling books in Farberville."

Luanne gave me a stricken look. "Oh, Claire, Dick didn't mean to imply you were butting in. He was up all night with Gannet."

"I realize that," I said, noting that she was not only telling lies to Mr. Right, but also offering his excuses and apologies. "All the same, if you'll draw me a map to the highway, I'll head back to town so Caron can work on her tan. Thanks for the drink."

"Did someone say 'drink'?" said a woman as she came around the corner of the house. "I would die for a Bloody Mary, easy on the salt, heavy on the vodka." She had shoulder-length ash-blond hair and slightly feline features accented by deftly applied makeup. Her pastel-pink lipstick matched the floral print of her jacket and trousers. Sunlight sparkled on gold earrings and a bracelet. Had she lifted her left hand, I was quite sure we'd be blinded from the glare off the massive diamond on her fourth finger.

"I thought I'd drop by on my way for yet another dreary meeting with the insurance agent," she said as she came onto the deck. At this distance I could see that she was superbly preserved rather than youthful; she undoubtedly visited her plastic surgeon more often than I did my gynecologist.

Dick rose and headed for the makeshift bar. "Luanne, you met Agatha Anne last week at the lodge. Claire Malloy, this is Agatha Anne Gallinago, president of the Dunling Foundation and wife of Sid, who happens to be my partner in the office and on the golf course. Be exceedingly leery of her or you'll find yourself stuffing envelopes and lecturing schoolchildren about the wonders of predatory birds."

Agatha Anne wiggled her fingers at Luanne, then crossed the deck to inspect me more closely. "I've heard of you! I absolutely loved all those stories about how you outwitted the police and solved their cases while they bumbled around like overgrown puppies. Are you here to help Dick?"

"I came for lunch," I said stiffly.

Agatha Anne smiled as if I'd dazzled her with my wit, then went to Luanne and squeezed her hand. "Livia said you looked terribly upset this morning, but who wouldn't after the Gestapo banged on the door in the middle of the night. You must have been a wreck the entire time Dick was being beaten with rubber hoses at that wretched man's jail." She took a glass from Dick and sank regally into a convenient chair. "Did they beat you with rubber hoses, darling, or has Gannet progressed to cattle prods?"

"Rubber hoses all the way," he said. "I'm going to take a shower before lunch. Claire, please stay and eat with us. If I said anything that offended you, I truly apologize, and if it'll help to make amends, I can put a finger in your mouth and you

can chomp down on it. Many of my patients find
it gratifying."

I declined to bite and agreed to stay. Once he
was gone, Luanne supplied me with a fresh drink
and I sat down across from Agatha Anne. She reminded me of Sally Fromberger, an indefatigable
woman with an innate need to organize those of
us who are terminally disorganized. She and Agatha Anne had the same carnivorous glint, the
same appraising smile. Both were likely to have
been born with clipboards in their tiny fists.

"You are going to help Dick, aren't you?" she
said.

"He doesn't seem to want my help."

Luanne gave me yet another stricken look.
"Someone has to do something before he goes
berserk and confesses to everything from the de-
struction of the Berlin Wall to Hurricane An-
drew."

Agatha Anne leaned forward and in a con-
spiratorial voice said, "Poor Dick is falling apart
right in front of us. Sid says the office staff are
threatening to quit if Dick doesn't start concentrating on his patients. It's so difficult to find
good dental technicians, especially ones willing
to work with children. There are days when I call
and can't tell whether the patients or their moth-
ers are sobbing more loudly in the background."

"All right," I said, albeit grudgingly, "you can
tell me about the accident, but after lunch I'm

going back to town. I have cartons to unpack and invoices to decipher."

I was not especially surprised when Agatha Anne took off with the fervor of an evangelist. "The Dunling Foundation is a nonprofit corporation which controls a four-thousand-acre bird sanctuary. Livia and Wharton donated the land and the use of the lodge, but we rely on fund-raisers to cover our yearly operations. Last year we netted nearly two hundred thousand dollars, one hundred percent of which went for our projects. We're very proud of the fact that no one on the board takes so much as a nickel in salary or even reimbursements for out-of-pocket expenses. It adds to our credibility in the community."

"What are your projects?" I asked politely, since I was sure she was going to tell me anyway.

"Mostly educational things like providing programs in the public schools, distributing material to civic groups, arranging barge tours for interested groups who want to see the eagles in their natural habitat. We also sponsor a treatment facility for wounded birds and animals. Anders Hammerqvist does a marvelous job patching up wings and broken legs. He's lived here for a good twenty years, and was doctoring animals as a matter of conscience when the Dunlings persuaded him to apply for a license and work for the foundation." She gave me a stern look. "Only licensed facilities can take in endangered species."

I felt as though I'd been accused of harboring

eagles in my bedroom. For the record, I actively dislike dogs and cats, but I've always liked birds, particularly the kind one watches from a sofa in a living room—rather than the kind that one stalks through thorny, tick-infested undergrowth. Eagles appeared to belong to the second category, but thus far no one had suggested I take a hike. "I understand Becca became a volunteer," I said to nudge her back into a more intriguing narrative.

Agatha Anne's fervor faded, and she sat back in the chair. "Becca was so young and vivacious that we were all amazed when she voiced an interest in our work. She had beautiful golden-blond hair, wide gray eyes, a perfect figure, and an irresistible smile. She was always so generous and cooperative that we were in awe of her. We simply adored her. Dick did, too."

"How did they meet?" Luanne asked as she stirred her drink with a piece of celery and affected indifference.

"Becca came three summers ago to stay with Scottie and Marilyn Gordon, who have the house on the second road past ours. She and Jan—Dick's first wife—hit it off immediately. They went into town for lunch several times a week and played tennis so often that I finally had to speak to Jan about her responsibilities in the office. She did the books and paid bills, and we were beginning to get nasty notes from some of our suppliers. Jan was dark and unpretentious, but she radiated beauty in her own quiet way. Late that summer she drowned in a tragic accident. Jillian dropped out of school for a semester, and Dick talked about selling this house because of the memories. Sid and I were dreadfully worried about him."

"And this tragic accident?" I prompted her.

"Jan loved to swim in the moonlight. There'd been a party. Dick rarely drinks too much, but this particular night he admitted he passed out the minute he hit the pillow. When he awoke several hours later, Jan was gone. He found her clothes in a pile near the edge of the water and called the sheriff's department and the lake patrol. They found the body shortly after dawn. The coroner ruled it an alcohol-related accident."

I thought it over for a moment. "Was there any reason to suspect foul play? Did she often swim when she'd been drinking?"

"She usually persuaded Dick or Jillian to swim with her," Agatha Anne said, for the first time sounding uncomfortable. "On that particular night, Jillian had gone to bed with a summer cold, and as I said, Dick was in no condition to join her. They did a blood test and determined that her alcohol level was twice the legal limit. They also found an empty brandy decanter near her clothes."

"But Captain Gannet wasn't satisfied," I said, watching Agatha Anne carefully. "That's part of the reason he's continuing to investigate the second accident."

"Dick didn't have an alibi—but how could he? Jillian had taken the type of heavy-duty antihistamines that come with the warning about operating heavy machinery, and it took him five minutes to rouse her after he called the police."

"And it happened more than three years ago," I said. "If anyone had noticed anything, surely he or she would have come forward by now."

"There was nothing to notice," Luanne muttered.

Agatha Anne perched on the arm of Luanne's chair to pat her shoulder. "Of course there wasn't. Sid and I have known Dick since we were in college together twenty-five years ago. The idea of Gannet suspecting him makes me ill. I spoke to the sheriff, but he's one of those fat, greasy politicians who's more concerned with the next election than the mental well-being of a handful of rich people who vote in another county. Sid even offered to make a donation to his campaign fund, but the sheriff cackled like a wild turkey."

I didn't point out that turkeys reputedly gobbled, because I feared an onslaught of ornithologically correct specifics. "Tell me about Becca's accident."

"It was half an hour after sunset on the final Friday in March," Agatha Anne said, wrinkling her forehead just enough to convey her scrupulous attempt to be precise without endangering her flawless complexion. "Georgiana and I went to Anders's trailer to discuss the release date for a red-tailed hawk that some ignorant chicken farmer had shot with a crossbow. Dick and Sid were in town. I came home at six-thirty and found a message from Becca on my answering machine. She said she was going out to Little Pine Island because of a report that an eagle was hurt. I drove to the marina, but just as I reached the dock, the boat exploded." She buried her face in her hands and shivered. When at last she spoke, her voice was husky and laden with pain. "There was a horrible red ball of fire and clouds of black smoke. Bits and pieces of the boat came splashing down as if they'd been hurled from heaven. There was no hope whatsoever of recovering what might have remained of the body."

"And you saw Becca on the boat?" I asked.

"Oh, yes, she was standing up while she drove, as she always did, with her hair streaming behind her and a can of diet soda in her hand. Bubo had seen her jump into the boat, and he was at the end of the dock yelling at her when I arrived. If only he'd been a little quicker, he could have stopped her, but he was inside selling bait or swilling beer or whatever he does to justify his salary."

"Bubo Limpkin is the manager of the marina," Luanne added in explanation. "He's a despicable excuse for a human being. Dick said they've tried to get him fired every summer since he came five years ago, but he sobers up and wheedles the owner into giving him one more chance."

I looked at Agatha Anne, who was checking

her reflection in the mirror of a gold compact. "And you'd reported a suspicious odor to him that same day?"

She snapped the compact shut and dropped it into her pocket. "That's right. I'd thought about taking the boat out that morning, but there was a faint odor in the cabin. I hunted down Bubo and told him to check the propane tanks, and he said he would."

"You didn't tell anyone else?" I asked.

"I mentioned it to Georgiana, but Becca had gone into town and it didn't occur to me that she might be using the boat later that same day. The Dunlings never take out the boat without first consulting me. They're terribly considerate, considering it was their money that funded the foundation and paid for the boat."

"But don't forget the quiche," Dick said as he came onto the deck, dressed in a fresh shirt and shorts. His face was smooth and his hair combed, but his eyes were still red and his eyelids puffy from a night of sleeplessness. "The fact that it was quiche rather than a meatball or a carrot stick really bugs Gannet. He's convinced we get dressed in tuxedos and mink coats and stand around sipping champagne, stuffing ourselves with caviar, and making fun of the local rubes. He looked distinctly skeptical when I told him Wharton had already started the charcoal for hamburgers when Becca lost her temper." He went to Luanne and put his arm around her waist. "The lasagna is bubbling, so perhaps we might set the table soon. Agatha Anne, you will be joining us, won't you?"

She shook her head. "I really do have to sign papers at the insurance office. The claims people have been dragging their heels all along, to the point I had to threaten to call our attorney." She offered me a manicured hand that had never probed an alien mouth. "I do hope we'll see you again, Claire. This has been such a thrill for me. I feel as though I've finally met Nancy Drew."

I was about to offer an equally insincere reply when we heard a gunshot.

3

I hurried to the rail and searched for the source of the shot. Sailors and skiers were eyeing the shore with appropriate alarm, and a pair of fishermen were frantically reeling in their lines in preparation to flee the cove. The birds that had been at the Dunling Lodge feeders were well on their collective way to the far side of the lake.

"It sounded close by," I said, wondering why the others were still seated and more interested in their drinks than in a potential homicide.

Agatha Anne laughed. "Wharton has declared war on a groundhog that lives near his vegetable garden on the other side of the lodge. He's tried all manner of traps and poisons, and even attached a hose to the exhaust pipe of his car and tried to asphyxiate the creature in its burrow. The day he tried dynamite has become a local legend. Lately, he's been crouching behind a bush with a shotgun. Livia's furious because the noise frightens away the birds and terrifies the hikers, but Wharton is beyond listening to her or anyone else. Nobody dares use the G-word in his presence."

"Wharton misses the good old days," Dick added, "when the enemy had the courtesy to stand up and offer himself as a target. This groundhog plays dirty. The garden is enclosed by a chainlink fence, three strands of electrified wire, and a final buffer of concertina wire. With the addition of guard towers and spotlights, it could serve as a prison camp. None of us could steal a tomato if we were starving, but the groundhog never misses a meal and seems to thrive on whatever poison Wharton feeds it. Livia swears it must weigh twenty pounds."

I studied the yard around Dunling Lodge, but no one clad in camouflage was on the prowl with a shotgun. "Your group doesn't object?" I asked Agatha Anne.

"Wharton's groundhog is the only one that's endangered. They're pests and have been known to spread rabies. I must run along to the claims office. If you encounter Wharton, for God's sake don't wiggle your nose and whistle at him." She went down the steps and around the corner of the house.

Luanne mumbled something about silverware and went inside. Dick waited until the sliding glass door was closed, then perched on the rail beside me and said, "Now that you've heard the details, can you pick out the clue that will exonerate me?"

"Both of the incidents sound like accidents," I said with a shrug. Despite his relaxed smile, there was an edge to him, an undertone of anxiety in both his voice and his demeanor. It didn't seem likely that he'd been involved with his wives' deaths, but I wasn't pleased with Luanne's mindless denial. I'd encountered congenial murderers in the past, from college students to white-haired teachers who were benignly cleansing the community of undesirables. For all I knew, the man sitting by me might find divorce a morally abhorrent way to end a marriage. However, for Luanne's sake, I forced myself to return his smile. "Surely Captain Gannet will find other crimes to occupy himself."

"I doubt it. He's obsessed with my guilt, and convinced that eventually he'll find proof or I'll break down and confess. He's probably building a gallows in his backyard in anticipation of the happy day."

"It's too bad that you and Becca had an argument the previous night, and in front of witnesses. I heard she nailed you with a piece of quiche."

"Quiche Lorraine, to be precise."

I gave him a chance to elaborate (not on the recipe, but on the gist of the argument), but he looked out at the lake with a faint frown. Luanne returned with a stack of plates and utensils, and I abandoned the rail to help her set the table.

We ate lunch and managed to talk about Farberville politics and the omnipresence of the weather. After Dick excused himself to watch a baseball game on television, Luanne and I carried plates and bowls into the kitchen.

"Well?" she said as she began to load a dishwasher imposing enough to be found in a busy restaurant.

I put the remains of the salad in a vast refrigerator, noting the plethora of fancy cheeses and champagne bottles competing for space with low-fat yogurt cartons and six-packs of designer water. No doubt the cases of caviar were kept in the pantry.

"Well, what?" I said. "The first accident happened three years ago, and the second three months ago. Even if I were inclined to nose around, I wouldn't find a smoking gun. The police have already scooped up whatever clues there were. The coroner has pronounced the deaths to be accidental. I'm sorry that Dick is being dogged by this Gannet, but there's nothing I can do about it."

To my horror, she began to sniffle. Seconds later she was sniveling and wiping her nose on a linen napkin. "I know I'm acting like a teenager, but what I feel is more than a goofy crush. I'm in love with Dick. I swore off marriage a long time ago, but now I lie awake at night trying to decide what to wear at the wedding and whether to ask Jillian to be the attendant. Should we honeymoon in Hawaii or Montreal? Will I ever learn how to operate his microwave? Can I feign pleasure in televised sports?"

"You've known him for all of three weeks, Luanne—and you're not acting like a teenager. Caron and Inez would find your behavior hopelessly infantile." I crossed my arms and glared at her like a proper British nanny in the doorway of the nursery. "Just let this relationship progress at a reasonable pace. He seems to be a nice man, and at some point the investigation will fizzle and his performance in the sack will meet your expectations again."

"You're about as romantic as this dirty glass," she said as she held up the offending object.

"Peter would be the first to agree. His latest ruse was an invitation for a Caribbean cruise. He gave me some altruistic nonsense about going to chaperon his mother, but I could see through his pathetic ploy."

"The man's a monster," Luanne said as she finished loading the dishwasher and inspected the countertops for an errant crumb that, she admitted ruefully, might offend Jillian. We returned to the deck, but neither of us was in the mood to talk. I finally asked her to draw me a map, thanked her for lunch, and went to my car. As I braked at the top of the driveway to prop my map on the dashboard, I heard another gunshot.

It was followed by an enraged bellow that included the phrase "you hairy bastard" and a rather picturesque string of expletives. It was not difficult to deduce the groundhog was alive and well—fed, that is.

I made it back to Farberville without incident and parked in the gravel lot next to the Book Depot. College students rolled by on bicycles and in cars with blaring radios, all apparently content to enjoy the sunny afternoon without the intrusion of literature. A beer bottle sailed over the fence of the beer garden and shattered on the railroad tracks. The only birds in sight were scruffy pigeons outside the health food café.

Caron and Inez were playing cards by the cash register, which was preferable to shrieking tidbits of prurient prose. I continued to a rack in a dim corner and found a bird book.

"Eagles winter in this area from December through March," I announced to the girls as I scanned the pertinent entry, "then return to Alaska and areas of northern and eastern Canada to breed. They were selected as a national symbol by Congress in 1782, but were hunted to near extinction in 1940 by Western ranchers, who thought they posed a threat to livestock, and by fishermen in the Northwest, who worried about salmon. Their population has been seriously depleted in the last few decades because they eat dead fish, which has caused them to absorb large amounts of pesticides. This interferes with their calcium metabolism and results in thin-shelled and often infertile eggs."

Caron snapped down a card. "How utterly fascinating, Mother. I can only pray that an eagle will not mistake my pale skin for that of a bloated perch and swoop down to rip out my eyeballs with its talons. It's your play, Inez. Stop dithering and do something."

"I'm thinking." Inez took a card from her hand, wrinkled her nose, and replaced it. As she reached for another, her martyred opponent sighed.

I turned the page. "The red-tailed hawk, commonly but erroneously called a chicken hawk, is a much-maligned species. It rarely eats poultry, but instead prefers rodents. Its cry is similar to yours."

"Gin," Inez said guardedly.

Caron threw down her cards and gestured imperiously for Inez to put them away. "What's that supposed to mean, Mother?"

"It produces a high-pitched descending scream with a hoarse quality," I said, squinting at the print. I'd vowed not to succumb to reading glasses until I turned forty. Said birthday loomed within a matter of months, as did Caron's sixteenth. I'd been treated to quite a few high-pitched descending screams involving her desire to drive a shiny red convertible to school on the first day—and my inability to buy her so much as a vintage Volkswagen. This reminded me of another source of friction. "Did you find out about driver's ed?"

I asked her. "The insurance agent says it'll save ten percent a year on the premium."

"My mother called the school last week," Inez said as she put the deck of cards in a drawer and closed it silently. Caron, when motivated to close a drawer, invariably slams it. "My parents are going to make me take it, too. They probably won't let me drive until I'm eighteen, but they want me to start practicing now."

"I think it's a waste of time," Caron said, "but if you want to pay one hundred and seventy-eight dollars so that I can drive around in a Chevrolet with a bunch of nerds, it's fine with me."

I shut the bird book and sat down on the stool behind the counter. "It costs money?"

"One hundred and seventy-eight dollars," Inez repeated for her best friend's witless mother. "My mother was pretty mad about it, but Coach Scoter explained that driver's ed isn't a mandatory part of the curriculum and the school board thinks—"

"As if the school board ever thinks," Caron said as she shoved Inez toward the door. "Let's go watch the last half of the college baseball game. We'll have to walk All The Way to the stadium, but we can sit behind the dugout and ogle the players."

"Wait a minute," I said in my steeliest maternal voice. "I can't afford to pay for this, especially while business is so bad."

"Suit yourself. I never expressed any desire to

drive around in a Chevrolet with a bunch of nerds. Rhonda Maguire wasn't forced to take driver's ed, and right after she passed the test, her mother just gave her the car key and some money for gas."

"Rhonda Maguire's mother has nothing to do with this," I said while I hunted in the drawer for a bottle of aspirin. "You have to take this course, and you'll have to find the money yourself. How much is in your savings account?"

"You're making me pay to be humiliated?" She was going to elaborate, but Inez whispered something to her and her incipient outrage was replaced with calculation. "Look, I'll do this Chevrolet thing if you insist, but I have less than twenty dollars in my savings account. I'm baby-sitting tonight for the Verdins, but I'll be lucky if they pay me more than ten dollars. They're more miserly than you are."

"I am not miserly, dear. I simply don't have a place in the budget for an unexpected one hundred and . . . whatever it is."

"Seventy-eight dollars," Inez contributed.

"Seventy-eight dollars," I said with a groan. "Business is always slack in the summer, and I'm behind with several publishers already. One of them has threatened me with a collection agency. You'd better find yourself a job to earn the money."

"I'm supposed to earn the money?" gasped Caron. The idea was enough to send her staggering into Inez, who yelped but held her ground.

"The baseball team already has a batboy, so I guess that's out. Shall I try to get on a road crew and spread hot tar in the blazing sun?"

"I hear the pay's quite good," I said. "Having a job won't ruin the remainder of your life. I'm sure you can find something less laborious than spreading hot tar if you develop a positive attitude."

Her lower lip shot out. "Okay, this positively sucks."

I retreated to my office. Shortly thereafter, the bell above the front door jangled, and I was left alone to ponder this newest financial tribulation while I pawed through drawers and boxes of junk in search of an aspirin. I wondered what it would be like to be able to volunteer my time to a charitable organization rather than work twelve hours a day to pay the rent. Agatha Anne had no need to reimburse herself for expenses, and I was certain she had a gold pillbox filled with aspirin. She would know exactly where it was, too.

Peter was off at a training session, and Luanne was on the deck at Turnstone Lake, so I spent the rest of the weekend peddling books and listening to Caron whine about my revolutionary (read: revolting) suggestion that she earn money rather than spend it. Child labor laws, the Emancipation Proclamation, Ebenezer Scrooge, and Rhonda Maguire's mother dominated the diatribes.

On Monday morning she announced that she was going to the unemployment office in order to find a squalid and demeaning job, although I suspected she had hopes that she might qualify in some obscurely logical way for unemployment benefits. Inez followed dutifully, and I was reading a guide to money management and wishing I had some to manage when they burst into the store an hour later.

"I have a fabulous job!" Caron announced as she swaggered past me and into the office, where I occasionally stash cans of soda. "I'll make plenty of money to pay for that stupid course," she yelled as things rattled and banged, "and have enough left over to buy a new bathing suit. There's a neat string bikini on sale at the mall."

I frowned at Inez, who was hovering by the mystery section. "Why did Caron change her mind about driver's ed?"

"Louis has to take it this summer," she said so softly I could barely hear her. "His sister told me he's signed up for the second semester."

"And Rhonda won't be sitting in the backseat between us," Caron said as she appeared in the doorway, her empty hands indicative of the futility of her mission. This in no way diminished her ebullient mood. "We have to endure a bunch of films about seat belts and drunken drivers, then Coach Scoter has everybody pile in the car and we take turns driving around town. Wouldn't it be a hoot if we saw Rhonda at a stoplight and waved at her? It'll be worth a hundred and seventy-eight dollars to see her choke."

"And how are you earning this?" I asked, worried that I was to hear about her "fabulous job" as a stripper.

Caron paused to savor the drama of the moment, then said, "I've been hired as a facilitator."

"A facilitator? What are you going to facilitate?"

"Oh, things," she said as she disappeared behind the science fiction rack. "Where are the bird books?"

"In the corner by the how-to's," I said, although we both knew she was as familiar with the layout as I. I was going to grill Inez, but she'd wandered out of sight. I waited impatiently until Caron reappeared with a book and an insufferably smug expression. "I didn't realize you had a secret ambition to become a bird fancier, dear. It's a wonderful hobby, but expensive. You need binoculars, along with bug repellent and heavy shoes in case you step on a snake. The pith helmet is optional."

"I'm going to be an official facilitator for some organization that frets about its feathered friends. On weekends, they used to do these programs where people pay money to goggle at birds, but this year they weren't going to hire anybody. They changed their minds yesterday, because they saw an adult eagle in a 'feeding posture,' whatever that is, way at the end of one of the creeks. It's the first successful nesting attempt on Turnstone Lake in modern times, so it's a big deal. Some guy paddled

down there and saw the aerie, which is supposedly the size of our bathroom. Now they've
blocked access to the creek, and the only way to
look at the eagles and eaglets is to go on a tour
with an official facilitator. Luanne isn't sure about
my duties, but it's likely that I'll drive a barge and
give lectures to the passengers. Therefore, I don't
have to worry about bugs or snakes—just boring
old farts in polyester shorts."

Inez peered around a rack. "I'm going to be
one, too, Mrs. Malloy. Mrs. Bradshaw says we'll
make ten dollars an hour once we've been
trained."

I was not amused. "Just how did this happen?
Was Luanne standing at the curb passing out applications to everybody who came by, or did the
unemployment agency sign you up?"

"We were walking by her store on the way to
the unemployment office," Caron said as she studied a menacing photograph of an eagle. "I went in
to ask her if she needed a clerk, and she mentioned this facilitator thing. She acted like you
knew all about it. We have to stay at some lodge
this weekend so a lady named Agatha Christie can
do this two-day training session. You're supposed
to come, too, but Luanne says you can stay at her
friend's house if you want. We start getting paid
the very next weekend. Eight hours a day for two
days and we can quit right then, but we may do
another weekend so I won't have to wear rags
when I'm driving around with Louis." She flipped

to a page with an equally menacing photograph of a great horned owl. "Yikes!"

To think I'd sipped beer and shared nachos with such a treacherous woman. I had no doubt Luanne and her new friend Agatha Anne had cooked up the scheme over a bottle of champagne and dollops of caviar on trimmed triangles of toast. "I fear I must decline Luanne's hospitality," I said. "I promised myself to update the inventory list this weekend. Inez, why don't you see if one of your parents can drive you to the lake?"

"They're going to a library conference in Santa Fe," she said. "Caron was supposed to ask you if I can stay with her this weekend."

"It's only Monday," Caron said without looking up. "I hope we're not going to have to get personal with the birds. It's one thing to talk about them, but I'd just as soon eat mouse guts as touch one."

Inez ventured to the counter. "My aunt had a parakeet once. It was kind of cute and liked to perch on the mantel and watch everybody. One afternoon the cat ate it. My aunt almost fainted when she came home and found little blue feathers all over the room."

"Big deal," Caron said crossly, turning the page. "Peregrine falcons can plunge at an estimated rate of one hundred and eighty miles an hour to snatch a duck out of the air. They could probably get your aunt's cat if they wanted to."

"She accidentally backed over it in the garage."

Caron flipped to another page. "Then she should have set it out for the turkey vultures. They locate carrion by smell. Black vultures, on the other hand, rely on their vision. Did it smell worse than it looked?"

I went to the office, slammed the door, and dialed the number of Secondhand Rose. "That was underhanded," I said when Luanne answered. "I refuse to be manipulated like this. You can be the transportation facilitator and drive the girls to the lake for the weekend. I'm staying right here in a bird-free environment."

"Captain Gannet showed up again Saturday, this time while we were having dinner with Agatha Anne and Sid. Dick had to go to the sheriff's office for an hour, but no one felt like eating when he got back. He barely said a word yesterday, and just dropped me off on the sidewalk when we got back to Farberville."

"A little petulant on his part."

"It's not petulance, Claire. It's been three months since Dick's felt as if he could finish a meal or sleep through the night without Gannet pounding on the door. Won't you please come this weekend and just talk to people? Someone may remember a scrap of information that'll prove the explosion was an accident. Then you can sail away in triumph and I can resume a serious study of the microwave manual."

I hung up but remained in the office, not sure if the dietary habits of vultures were an improvement over petunias of passion and lilies of lust. A vision of a moonlit deck drifted into my mind. A starry sky, the distant sound of music, the salty breeze, the tinkle of silver and crystal. And Peter Rosen doing his best to convince me to choose a date to book a justice of the peace. His nose is a bit beakish, and his gaze can be as piercing as that of an eagle or a hawk. His hands are manicured but as strong as talons.

I realized I was beginning to feel like the heroine in Hitchcock's *The Birds*.

4

I remained steadfast for the ensuing forty-eight hours, during which Luanne called approximately forty-eight times to beseech me to change my mind. She solemnly swore that the Dunling Foundation hired high school and college students every summer to serve as facilitators, and although this year they'd intended to cut back on staff, the discovery of the aerie would bring in bird-watchers from across the state. Agatha Anne was desperate.

It was no champagne-and-caviar conspiracy, Luanne insisted. She made blunt remarks about the high cost of driver's ed and the moral irresponsibility of allowing an unschooled driver onto the streets. Friendship and fidelity were topics explored more than once. More appeals were made than the Supreme Court receives in a term.

I resisted forty-seven times, then finally agreed to take the girls to the lake on Friday and spend the night at Dick's house, although I was determined to return to Farberville the following morning and sell books for the remainder of the weekend. That I could do so without periodic eruptions from my daughter had as much influence on my capitulation as Luanne's banalities.

We arrived at Turnstone Lake shortly after six o'clock. Caron and Inez each had a bulging duffel bag and an assortment of overnight cases with their precious hair equipment and makeup. They'd become increasingly apprehensive as we drove down the narrow roads, and their conversation shifted from their anticipated wealth to the possibility that they might be coerced into the woods, where they would be at the mercy of poisonous snakes and ravenous bears.

"That's the driveway to Dick Cissel's house," I said as we drove by the gate and continued toward Dunling Lodge. "It's just across the cove from where you'll be staying. You could get there in less than five minutes if you walked along the edge of the water."

"And managed not to step on a water moccasin," Caron said, her lower lip quivering with despair. From under a much-crinkled brow, she scowled at her surroundings. "I thought there'd be more houses and stores and less of this forest stuff. How can people stand to stay out here? What do they do all day—gather nuts and berries?"

"They enjoy nature, I suppose," I said as I

braked to allow a squirrel to dart across the road. "Considering your opinion of things that scuttle, scamper, or fly, you might have thought a little harder before you accepted the job."

"Scuttle?" Inez said from the backseat.

I declined to define my terms and drove down a steep road to Dunling Lodge. A weathered sign proclaimed it to be the headquarters of the Dunling Foundation Bird and Wildlife Sanctuary, founded 1984. Smaller letters acknowledged that escorted tours were available from July through March, but hikers were always welcome and information could be procured in the lodge. Donations were appreciated, but not required. Alcoholic beverages were expressly forbidden, as was littering.

There were several cars and trucks in the rocky parking area. As I rolled to a stop, a quartet of sturdy people emerged from a path into the woods and began to unload gear into a station wagon. Gender was not obvious, but all had sunburned faces, binoculars, bird guides, and bulging backpacks. When a second group emerged, there was good-natured repartee about such curious topics as wigeons and gallinules.

The lodge may have been a romantic honeymoon destination at one time, but from this closer perspective I could see the broken windows in the upper two floors, the bare mortar where rocks had fallen, the obvious tilt of the porch roof above a massive wooden door. Glass sparkled in the ground-floor windows, however, and trellises were thick with honeysuckle on either end of the porch. The yard was untamed, the weeds high, the trees and shrubs allowed to sprawl according to the dictates of nature. Poles of varying heights held aloft birdhouses, and at the farthest one, attempted trespassing was being thwarted by squawks and a great deal of fervent flapping.

I was debating whether to mention the bat colony when Caron said, "I've changed my mind. I'll get a job washing dishes at the Mexican restaurant. It pays minimum wage, but I can work twelve hours a day. Maybe they'll let me make tacos after I've been there for a while. Making tacos can be very fulfilling, I hear."

"Mrs. Verdin wants a baby-sitter on Thursday mornings so she can play bridge," Inez added. "She doesn't even pay minimum, though. You'd be baby-sitting for the twins until they leave for college."

"Forget it," I said sharply, although I was inwardly aglow with petty pleasure at their distress. "You agreed to this training session, and you're not going to back out just because you're not staying at the Hilton. The first floor has been remodeled. You'll be perfectly comfortable."

With a screech, Caron slithered onto the floorboard and covered her head with her arms. It seemed an overly melodramatic response to my dictum, and I was about to say as much when I spotted a man near the corner of the house. He was cradling a shotgun, the barrel of which was pointed in our general direction.

"Don't worry about Wharton Dunling," I said with a great deal more assurance than I inwardly felt. "He has a problem with a groundhog that's been ravaging his garden. He won't shoot us unless we go after his zucchini."

I waved at him to convince myself, if not the girls, that he was harmless. He was tall and bony, with cadaverous cheeks, protruding ears, and a tight mouth. He was nearly bald, and what hair remained on the sides of his head quivered like white pinfeathers. His days of wearing a crisply starched uniform had passed, obviously. He wore baggy plaid shorts, a stained T-shirt, and moccasins. His legs were hairy and white, his bare ankles gnarly.

In response to my gesture, he stepped out of view.

Caron peeked over the edge of the dashboard. "He must feel right at home in this place," she muttered as she resumed her seat and twisted the rearview mirror to make sure she hadn't sustained damage. "He probably was killed in the Crimean War. I can hardly wait to be kept awake all night by rattling chains and guttural groans. There's not much point in worrying about driver's ed, is there? In the morning I'll be found at the foot of the stairs." She sprawled across the seat, clutched her throat, and widened her eyes in fabricated terror. "Tell my mother"—gurgle,

gurgle—"that I forgive her. It wasn't Entirely Her Fault." Her eyes fluttered closed and her hands dropped limply to the seat.

"Maybe we should have asked Mrs. Bradshaw more questions," said a small voice.

I opened the car door. "Get your luggage. Let's hope Mrs. Dunling is here. Perhaps she has cookies and milk waiting for you in her cozy kitchen."

Livia Dunling was hovering in the doorway when we extracted the luggage and staggered to the porch. She was wearing the same skirt and sweatshirt, and apparently had been wearing her hat earlier in the day, since her hair stuck out at odd angles. "Welcome, welcome, welcome," she said as she waved us inside. She sounded pleased to have guests, if a trifle puzzled about the identity of same.

"I'm Claire Malloy," I said. "We met last weekend when I was lost and you were on the trail of a woodpecker."

"Do you recall if I spotted him?"

"I don't think so. When I drove up, he flew away."

Livia absently scratched a welt on her neck. "I shall consult my list to see if I checked him off. Come along to the patio and we can all have a nice glass of lemonade. I don't know where Wharton is at the present, but I'm sure he'll turn up sooner or later."

We left the luggage by the door and followed her through a cavernous room with a few pieces of worn furniture in front of a rock fireplace. What had once served as a reception desk was now the repository for racks of pamphlets and postcards.

A separate rack held applications for membership in the Dunling Foundation, with its motto: "An Eagle Freed Needs a Friend Indeed." What said eagle truly needed, I thought, was a less poetic PR firm. Through a doorway I caught a glimpse of a dining-room table that was an insignificant island in a vast sea of mahogany paneling.

The patio was less daunting. Caron and Inez seemed heartened by the proximity of the lake and huddled together to assess the possibility of escape by motorboat. As Livia poured lemonade from a pitcher, I sat down on a redwood bench and let the breeze ruffle my hair. "You have a lovely view," I said.

"It's so kind of you to mention it. Wharton was in the army for thirty years, so we were constantly on the move, never staying anywhere long enough to put down roots. This is the first time I've been able to dedicate myself to a garden. Everything is chosen for its appeal to various birds and butterflies. The milkweed is for the monarchs, of course, so they can lay their eggs. The snapdragons and trumpet vine are for the dear little hummingbirds. The buckeyes are as mad for the daisies as the painted ladies are for the butterfly bush and bee balm."

I smiled politely before I glanced toward the

deck of Dick's house in hopes Luanne would come to the rescue. Lemonade has its place in the good ol' summertime, but I'd been in the car with the girls for well over an hour. That which appealed to this bookseller was a shot of scotch. The deck appeared to be uninhabited.

"Try these." Livia handed me a pair of binoculars. "I always do. Only last week I watched Jillian trying on a bathing suit. She looked like a puffed-up goshawk glaring at itself in the mirror. She is a very unhappy child, or perhaps I should say nestling."

I studied the house across the cove. There were two wineglasses on the rail, a jacket draped on the back of a chair, and a cordless telephone on a table. There were no visible bloodstains. The sliding glass doors were closed, and I could see no movement within the living room. Feeling a bit guilty but having great fun, I aimed the binoculars at the windows along the side of the house. The interiors were too dim to provide a proper inspection, but I could make out beds, a dresser here and there, the backs of chairs—and nary a body dangling from a noose.

"Who're you spying on?" Caron asked in a disapproving voice.

"Luanne, I hope," I said as I aimed the binoculars at the final window. Neatly centered in the rectangle was a silhouetted figure regarding me through binoculars. I hastily set Livia's down on the table and took a deep drink of lemonade.

"The nestling" had just as much right as I did to spy on the neighbors, I told myself as I struggled to swallow, and there was no reason to feel as if I'd been caught filching pennies from the collection plate.

"When do we get trained?" Inez asked Livia, who was nodding benevolently at a cardinal on a nearby feeder.

"After breakfast, I should think. Wharton and I eat out here when the weather permits. It's very peaceful without the motorboats, and the feeders are at their busiest. Only yesterday we had a visit from a flock of goldfinches. They do so love the sunflowers, as do the rufuous-sided towhees. It's such a joy to watch them."

Caron rolled her eyes at me as she picked up the binoculars. I held my breath until she directed them at a party barge overflowing with bronzed young men. She hissed at Inez, who yanked off her glasses and cleaned the lenses on her shirttail.

I had no desire to sit on the veranda and sip lemonade, but I was not enthusiastic about the prospect of arriving at Dick's house to be admitted by Jillian. It occurred to me that I could simply drive home, make myself a drink, and read the newspaper in solitude. Luanne would be furious, but I'd have until Monday to come up with a plausible excuse for my cowardliness.

"Oh, good, you're here," said Agatha Anne as she came out the back door, this time wearing the brand of jeans advertised in magazines I couldn't afford to read. Her T-shirt was emblazoned with the Dunling Foundation motto. She introduced herself to the girls, adding, "It's always heartening to meet young people who take an interest in the environment. Neither of my children did. Trey spent his summers playing in golf tournaments all over the state, and Melissa had such a crush on the tennis pro that she practically lived at the country club for three years."

"Did they take driver's ed?" Caron asked, giving me a sullen look meant to remind me of my responsibility for the current situation, which she no doubt found somewhere between dire and disastrous.

"Not that I recall," said Agatha Anne. "Why don't you come along with me and I'll show you our office here at the lodge and get you started on your study material. Normally I mail it several months in advance, but it wasn't possible this time and you may have to read well into the night. We are incredibly excited about the eagles at the far end of Blackburn Creek. If we can make them feel welcome, the three offspring may return and eventually we may have a thriving community of breeders. At the same time, we'll have a wonderful opportunity to educate the public about the vital role of raptors in the ecological complex."

Caron stiffened. "We thought we might go for a swim before it gets dark."

"There's no time to waste," Agatha Anna said sweetly. "Claire, would you like to see the office?

It's in a state of chaos as usual, but you might enjoy looking over our pamphlets and brochures. We just got in some splendid new material about the migratory pattern of the golden eagle."

"Did you?" said Livia, struggling to her feet. As she headed for the door, her limp was barely noticeable. "I must have a look."

Agatha Anne herded us through the living room and down a hallway to a door with a discreet brass plaque that proclaimed it to be the administrative residence of the Dunling Foundation, Inc. The office consisted of a large room, most likely a lounge in the hotel's heyday, with three cluttered desks, several tables piled high with boxes and folders, a row of file cabinets, and a bookshelf crammed with colorful brochures. Agatha Anne scooped up a foot-high stack of folders and thrust it into Caron's arms. Inez received a similar burden. I was honored with a glossy brochure, as was Livia, who immediately sat down behind the nearest desk and opened hers.

"I don't expect you to memorize all of this before tomorrow," Agatha Anne said to the girls as she noted their expressions. "We'll review it together, and then you can work on it again tomorrow night after dinner. There are two hundred and eighty known species of raptors, after all."

"Oh," Caron said, not sounding especially gratified to be enlightened. Inez merely blinked at the top of her stack.

Their slave driver smiled at me. "And I'll see you in half an hour, Claire. I must run home and get out of these dusty clothes before the party."

"Before the party?"

"Luanne and Dick have invited a few people for hamburgers. This will give us all a chance to get to know each other, won't it?" She laded the words with significance so that I, her personal effigy of Nancy Drew, would realize this was my opportunity to interrogate the suspects—except no one was supposed to be suspected of anything.

Livia tucked the brochure in her pocket, and for what seemed like the first time, noticed Caron and Inez. "You gals are staying here, aren't you? I'll have to think which bedrooms are clean. Wharton and I moved to the Purple Martin only three days ago, so I suppose you could take the Hummingbird if you don't mind sharing."

"You changed bedrooms three days ago?" asked Caron.

"Or maybe four. There are seven bedroom suites on this floor. Rather than deal with cleaning on a weekly basis, we work our way through all seven rooms and then have them cleaned at one time. Agatha Anne arranges for a service to come in once a month."

Caron and Inez did not respond, but I could tell from their faces that they found this less than enchantingly eccentric. I wondered if the Dunlings had done the same during their army years. Why clean the bathtub when one is to be transferred sooner or later?

"I'll see you girls in the morning," Agatha Anne chirped, waved, and was heading out the door when the telephone rang. She returned and picked up the receiver. "Dunling Foundation."

Livia curled a finger at the girls. "Come along and we'll get you settled. Would you prefer the Mockingbird? It's done in soothing shades of gray and white."

"It sounds great," Caron said lugubriously as she and Inez trudged toward the door. Neither felt compelled to wish me a festive evening at the party, but I was fairly sure they would not flee during the night.

"I don't know where Wharton is," Agatha Anne said into the receiver, "but I'll see if I can find him." She frowned, then said, "Fine, Wharton. I didn't realize you were on the line."

As soon as she'd replaced the receiver, I said, "I'll see you shortly."

"Please take some more literature, and do consider becoming a volunteer, Claire. Our biggest and most vital fund-raiser of the year, the Rapturous Raptors Ball, is coming up in less than a month. Becca was in charge of it, bless her heart, and now I have no idea who's lining up the orchestra and who has the list of donations for the silent auction. The invitations are ready to go out, but I still haven't found a volunteer to address the envelopes by hand. There are only a thousand. It really shouldn't take all that long." She regarded me as if assessing my skills in the genteel art of penmanship.

"I guess I'll head over to Dick's house," I said hastily. Without catching a glimpse of the girls (or hearing their mutters of indignation from within a birdcage), I retraced our path to the living room and went out the front door. I was not surprised to see a milk-chocolate-brown Jaguar beside my hatchback. Agatha Anne would not have driven a common species of car. I drove up the hill and down the driveway, and only as I cut off the engine did I remember who was apt to be the sole occupant. Taking my overnight bag from the backseat, I tried to decide if I ought to mention the mutual surveillance and laugh it off, or pretend it had never happened and cower in a guest room until Luanne arrived. If guests were expected in a matter of minutes, surely the host and hostess would be there as well.

I was dismayed when Jillian opened the door. "I'm Claire Malloy," I said, aware of a shrill edge to my voice. "I was here last weekend, but you were dashing off to the print shop. Is Luanne here?"

"She and Father went to the marina to get a bag of ice." She stepped back and waited while I came inside, then said, "I'll take your bag. Luanne said for you to make yourself a drink and wait on the deck. I'll bring some crackers and cheese in a minute.

Her lack of inflection was disconcerting; I'd stumbled across dead bodies with livelier expressions. "Don't go to any trouble," I said as I made myself walk serenely through the living room to the deck, where I noticed that the wineglasses, telephone, and jacket had vanished. A barbecue grill and a table holding the necessary tools had been set beside the bar. I made a drink, then settled down in a chair and looked toward the lodge for a bat—or Caron and Inez ducking from bush to bush as they made for the lake. The boats were gone, which meant they might have quite a lengthy swim.

Jillian came through the door and set down a tray. She poured herself a glass of soda water, sat down near me, and made a moderately successful attempt to smile. "Luanne said you own a bookstore."

Grateful for a safe topic, I rattled on about the history of the Book Depot and its current financial woes. She appeared to be listening, but her eyes were so small and recessed that it was difficult to gauge her reaction. I finally ran out of the smallest minutia, cast about for another safe topic, and said, "I understand you graduated last year."

"I should have graduated earlier, but I left school when Mother died. I stayed in counseling for two years afterward, trying to deal with my guilt. I wish Father had done the same, but he simply turned inward and refused to face reality. My grief made me stronger; his left him vulnerable."

"Vulnerable to what?"

"The kindness of strangers," she said darkly. "He was drunk the night of Mother's death. If he hadn't been, he would have dissuaded her from going for a swim, or at least accompanied her. She was all alone when she drowned. What a sad way to die. . . ."

"Agatha Anne said you'd taken an antihistamine that knocked you out," I murmured.

"I'd come down with a cold and was desperate to sleep. I certainly wouldn't have taken anything if I'd known Mother would get one of her crazy urges for a midnight swim on a night when Father was snoring out his brains." She went to the rail and pointed at the strip of rocky beach below the deck. "That's where her clothes were. It's not twenty feet from where I'm standing. She may have cried out when she realized she was in trouble, but no one was in any condition to hear her. She was all alone."

It was the second time she'd used the phrase, and I wondered if there was something more to it. When she failed to continue, I gently said, "As was Becca when the boat exploded. Your father has had terrible luck, hasn't he?"

"I hoped that she would help him with his

grief. She was young and vibrant, always laughing, teasing him to take a vacation or go to concerts and the theater, dropping by with steaks to grill or some gourmet delight she'd found in town. It was obvious to the rest of us that she was madly in love with him. One day he finally realized that she was there, and they were married within a week."

"Did you object?"

"Oh, no. I did all I could to take care of Father, but he's an adult and entitled to find happiness where he can. Becca was devoted to him." She stood up and started for the living room. "Becca was perfect," she said as she closed the door.

"Was she?" I said under my breath, then plastered on a smile as I heard voices from the side of the house. I recognized Agatha Anne's chirps, but neither the male nor the female speaker was familiar. Nor should they have been, I realized as she came onto the deck with a pudgy man and a woman with a frizzy cloud of light brown hair.

"Claire, this is Georgiana Strix and my husband, Sid," Agatha Anne said. "I've already told them all about you."

Sid was so impressed that he nodded before veering to the bar. He had a thick back, thinning hair, and a sunburned neck. When he turned around, I had a view of soft jowls and a fussy, effeminate mouth. The overall effect would have been comical, had it not been for his sharply appraising eyes. In contrast with Agatha Anne's

impeccably coordinated blouse and shorts, he
wore striped shorts and a garish shirt more suitable to the back nine of a Hawaiian golf course.
On his feet were black socks and sandals. "How
ya doing?" he said as he went into the house.

Georgiana was watching me with suspicion,
as if Agatha Anne had related stories about my
predilection for spontaneous violence. Almost
lost in the mass of frizziness, her face was that of
a puzzled ingenue—unnaturally colorless skin,
wide eyes, puffy lips, and a tiny wrinkle above
her upturned nose.

Agatha Anne clearly abhorred a verbal vac-
uum. "Georgiana is on the board of the Dunling
Foundation and handles all the accounts. I'll bet
you never would have guessed that she majored in
business administration and single-handedly ran a
great big medical clinic in Houston after she graduated. Her lake house is next to ours, and we just
borrow from each other day and night, don't we?"

"No, we don't," Georgiana said in a high voice.
"Sometimes I forget to pick up things at the store
in town, but most of the time I just make do.
Barry used to do the shopping; now I have to do
it. I try to keep a list." Abruptly her eyes filled
with tears and her voice soared even higher. "My
support group says that forgetting things like
lemons and margarine is symptomatic of my refusal to forget Barry. That's not right. I'd do anything to forget that son of a bitch!"

Agatha Anne swooped in with a tissue and

dabbed Georgiana's cheeks. "Now, honey, don't start on this. There's no reason for you to waste the time it takes to say his name. Would you like to lie down in the guest room for a minute?" Without waiting for a response, she led the trembling woman inside.

It may have been getting crowded inside the house (it seemed to be a popular destination), but it was peaceful on the deck. I was again searching for bats when Sid came back with a bowl of peanuts.

"I hear you're a private investigator," he said as he put cheese on a cracker and deftly conveyed it to his mouth. He flicked crumbs off his fingertips, then added almost incuriously, "You carry a gun?"

"In my back pocket."

He turned his attention to the peanuts. "What happened to Agatha Anne? You shoot her and stick the body under the deck?" He held up a hand that, like Dick's, had probed the mouths of countless children. I failed to spot any fresh teeth marks, but there were some suspicious scars. "I won't turn you in or anything. In fact, I'll take you out to dinner to express my gratitude. I know a great little country inn with fireplaces in the bedrooms."

"Georgiana became upset. Agatha Anne thought she should lie down in the guest room."

"That girl's gonna end up with bedsores. Dick has held up better than she has, and he was arranging funerals. She's just getting a divorce." Ever loyal, he returned to the cheese and crackers, although he was managing to drink steadily throughout the assault on the hors d'oeuvres. "From the way Georgie's carrying on, you'd think she was diagnosed with inoperable cancer. Sure, Barry's a nice guy, but she's attractive and there are other suckers out there. You're a widow, right? I'll bet you haven't spent too many nights alone in bed."

"I'm a widow with a gun," I said coldly.

He gave me a guileless, if somewhat cheesy, smile. "At least you know where your husband is. Georgie's problem is that she knew Barry was having another affair, but she couldn't figure out who the bimbo was or where they were getting it on. She kept us up till dawn for weeks while she agonized over hiring someone in your profession to get the evidence. Agatha Anne convinced her that it would cost a bundle and she'd still want a divorce in the end. My wife's what you call a pragmatist."

I ignored his jibe about my purported profession. "Divorce can be stressful."

"Barry seems to be holding up damn well. He took his share of the assets and bought a houseboat. Now he lives down in Key West, drinking rum and ogling college girls in bikinis. He was an investment broker, so I always thought he had an account on the side that Georgie never knew about. Helluva retirement, considering he's in his mid-forties. Surf, sun, and lots of sleek nubile skin."

While his ex-wife has a nervous breakdown, I thought but did not say. I made myself a drink, then went down the steps to the yard. There was a faint path through the high grass to the edge of the lake. I carefully made my way to the narrow swath of rocks where Dick's first wife had taken her swan swim in the moonlight.

From here I could see only the top story and roof of Dunling Lodge. Even if Wharton and Livia had been awake, they would have had to go beyond their patio and partway down the hill in order to see anything. And supposedly there'd been nothing to see except a woman slipping out of her clothes, finishing off a decanter of brandy, and easing out into the inky water. With that quantity of alcohol in her blood, she might have splashed about, but the sound would have been lost in the darkness.

I heard a footstep behind me. Hoping it was not the loathsome Sid, I looked over my shoulder. Dick regarded me for a moment, then said, "Investigating the scene of the crime?"

"Escaping from Sid, actually," I said as I picked up a rock and tossed it into the water. It sank with a tiny plop. Ripples formed, but within seconds the surface was as imperturbable as Dick's expression.

5

"But you have to go to the marina," Luanne whimpered as we struggled over my overnight bag like spoiled nursery-school children. We were in front of Dick's house, where our undignified dance was being observed only by a mockingbird perched on the chimney. It was not yet eight o'clock in the morning, but I wanted to go by my apartment and pick up the newspaper before I went to the Book Depot. A day without international crises—and a crossword puzzle—is like a day without sunshine.

I finally prevailed and tossed the bag in the backseat of my car. "No, I don't have to go to the marina. I don't have to do anything except go back to Farberville and open the store. Yesterday my horoscope said to anticipate an abundance of tangible assets today. I can't risk offending the planets."

"Captain Gannet ordered Bubo not to talk to any of us. You can pretend to be a reporter or even just a tourist who heard about the accident, then listen to his story. How long can it take?"

I consulted my watch. "Too long. Look, Luanne, I came here as promised and politely listened to Agatha Anne carry on about eagles and Georgiana about her ex-husband. I did not stick a fork in Sid's hand when he pinched my derrière, nor did I scream when I was hunting for a blanket and Jillian loomed behind me in the hallway like some character out of a bad movie. I was a model houseguest. Now I'm going to concentrate on being a model bookseller."

"Agatha Anne and I think there must be some wrinkle in Bubo's story that Gannet finds odd. I've tried several times to bring up the subject, but Bubo won't say a word about the day of the accident. Someone with your deviousness could get it out in no time flat."

"Deviousness? Is that to imply you regard me as a contemporary Ms. Machiavelli?"

Before she could offer an acceptable apology, Dick came to the door with the cordless telephone. "Claire, you have a call from your daughter. She sounds agitated. . . ."

I did not leap over the begonias, but instead reluctantly went around them to accept the telephone. "Hello, dear," I said.

"You have to come get us Right This Minute!" Caron whispered. "Otherwise, I may throw myself off the roof and splatter the parking lot with blood and guts and shards of splintered bone."

"Why would you do something potentially nauseating like that—and why are you whispering?"

"So She won't overhear me."

The line went dead, although I doubted Caron was likely to do the same anytime soon. I managed a wan smile for Luanne and Dick, who were watching me with understandable perplexity. "Caron's feeling a little low this morning," I said. "I suppose I'll stop by Dunling Lodge on my way back to town."

"And by the marina?" Luanne said brightly.

Ignoring her, I thanked Dick for his hospitality and drove to Dunling Lodge. The parking lot was unsullied. I parked near the Jaguar, patted my gallant little car on its slightly dented hood, and was about to step onto the porch when Caron and Inez darted from around the corner of the house, panting like escapees from a chain gang.

"What's going on?" I asked, startled.

Caron yanked me behind a trellis. "These people are deranged. Do you know what time we were forced to have breakfast? Do you?"

"At dawn," Inez volunteered.

"It's not like we were going to get any more sleep," continued Caron, who does not care to be interrupted in the midst of sinister recitations. "As soon as the sun came up, hordes of jabbery birds descended on the feeders like little Mongols. I put my pillow over my head, but then Mrs. Dunling came in and started jabbering, too. When they do an autopsy on her, they're going to discover she really does have a bird brain."

Inez leaned closer and said, "When I saw her in the hall this morning, she was flapping her arms. She said she was exercising, but I'm not so sure. When the moon is full, she probably sits in a tree and hoots with the owls."

Caron nudged her aside. "So we got up and went to the patio for breakfast, where she about had a coronary because she spotted a great spangled fritillary hovering in the vetch."

I sensed from her dramatic pause that a response was expected of me. "No kidding?" I said.

"She carried on like she'd seen the Secretary of the Treasury, but all I saw was a stupid butterfly. At least Mr. Dunling already had eaten and was down at the edge of the lake. He tests the water every morning for pesticides. If you ask me, he should be testing their tap water. I was expecting a bowl of worm flakes, but we had yummy bran turds instead. And tomato juice. You know how much I Absolutely Loathe tomato juice."

It was well past my designated time of departure. "I realize you're being brutalized, girls, but I need to go. Consider this as an opportunity to improve your survival skills. Luanne will bring you home tomorrow afternoon."

Caron sensed her chances for a timely rescue were dwindling and began to sniffle. "There was a whippoorwill under our bedroom window, Mother. Every five minutes from midnight until four o'clock, it made this ear-shattering sound. I seriously considered asking Mr. Dunling to loan me his shotgun so I could facilitate it straight to its celestial nest."

Inez shook her head. "Actually, it was a chuck-will's-widow. It makes this funny little chuckle at the beginning of its song." She pursed her mouth to demonstrate.

"Spare us an audition for the Audubon Society," Caron growled at her, then returned to the task at hand—eliciting pity. "Agatha Anne's in the office on the telephone, but she said when she's done, we're going on a hike to look for birds. I looked at pictures of birds last night until I thought my eyeballs were going to pop out of their sockets. Why would I want to see live ones? Do you know what birds are? They're reptiles with feathers! I'm supposed to go on a hike to look for flying lizards?"

"And there are something like eight thousand species of birds," Inez said. "Agatha Anne acts like we're supposed to be able to list them one by one, starting with accipiter." She flinched as Caron glared at her. "I just happened to notice it was first. It's a hawk."

"Everybody knows that," I said pretentiously, seizing the chance for a maternal power play. "Now, if you'll unhand me, you can go find out what's at the end of the list and I can go back to town. Make the best of it."

Caron's fingers dug in more tightly. "Okay,

we will make one last attempt to cooperate with that tyrant—if you agree to stay here until we get back from the hike. If you don't, we're going to pack our bags and walk back to the highway, where we can hitch a ride with some jerk with extravagant body hair and dirty fingernails. If he doesn't rape and kill us, we should be home in time for lunch."

Inez gulped. "We should?"

Caron released my arm in order to cross hers and stare at me. Her jaw may have trembled, but her voice did not as she said, "That's right."

For a brief moment, I tried to see her as a defenseless pink infant in a bassinet rather than a cold-hearted miscreant who could be recruited with equal fervor by the Mafia and the CIA. "No, that's blackmail. Besides, it must be five miles to the highway. You'll never make it, considering the amount of luggage you brought. You have a verbal contract with the Dunling Foundation and the obligation to hold up your end of it."

"Come on, Inez. I want to write my will before we pack. I think I'll leave everything to some organization that fights child abuse and neglect." Her lower lip shot out far enough to catch tears, had she been able to manufacture them. It was obvious she was trying.

I wished I had the nerve to get in my car and drive away without so much as a glance in the rearview mirror, but she sounded obstinate enough to follow through with her idiotic threat.

It might take them two hours or more to arrive at the highway (if they could find it), at which time they would be so exhausted and desperate that they might accept a ride in a truck with a gun rack and a cooler of beer. Images of what could happen flashed through my mind. They were less attractive than craven capitulation, I concluded grimly.

"All right, I'll stay until noon," I said. "You will display interest and enthusiasm, you will take notes, and you will search the branches for birds rather than the ground for snakes. If you are able to change your attitude and complete the training session, I'll overlook this. Then again, if you come back and insist I take you home, you won't need to worry about any unfriendly elements of nature until school starts in the fall because you will be grounded. Got that?"

"What about the one hundred and seventy-eight dollars for driver's ed?" she retorted with the polish of a practiced plea bargainer.

"I don't see how you can earn much money in your bedroom, but perhaps you can follow up on one of those magazine ads that promises hundreds of dollars a week for stuffing envelopes with unspecified material. Let's hope it's not pornography. In any case, it's irrelevant because you won't be able to take driver's ed, which means you won't be allowed to drive until after you take it next summer."

"Next summer? All the ninth-graders will be driving by then."

"I'll be here at noon," I said, then went to my car and drove up the driveway before the argument could escalate. As I paused at the top of the hill, I saw Dick and Luanne come out of his house and climb into the Rover like a suburban couple off to the hardware store. I had no desire to continue a conversation with Jillian, if she was still there. Nor did I have a desire to return to Dunling Lodge, where the idea of addressing envelopes was as repugnant as being mistaken for a groundhog. I took Luanne's map from the glove compartment, located the marina, and turned left.

After a few mistakes, I arrived at a squatty weathered building. A long dock ran alongside it, with three more jutting out like the cross strokes of an E. The farthest one was covered. Under the metal roof were cabin cruisers, party barges, elegant motorboats, and sailboats with neatly furled sails. A gas pump stood at one corner of the marina office, which was decorated with signs stating the availability of bait and beer. As I cut off the engine, a gangly boy carrying a quantity of each walked down the pier to a prosaic fishing boat, and he was pulling away as I stepped onto the dock and gloomily asked myself what on earth I was doing.

In the past, I had stumbled across a number of murders camouflaged as accidents. I'd searched for motives and opportunities, shrewdly interrogated suspects, and at least metaphorically crawled on the floor in search of clues—all to prove a murder had been committed. I had no idea how to prove one hadn't. For all intents and purposes, I was to assume everyone was telling the truth. There were no suspects, no clues, no motives or opportunities. There were no red herrings in Turnstone Lake. So what was I supposed to do?

To add to my exasperation, I was investigating a noncrime from three months earlier. It's not remarkably uncommon in mystery fiction, and some of my favorite sleuths have taken on cases in which the murders occurred decades earlier. Somehow, a few clues always remained, and a few convenient suspects were still alive. That, regrettably, was fiction. In real life, few of us can effortlessly remember events from the previous week, much less from months earlier. Bubo's reticence might lie in nothing more ominous than a substandard memory.

I walked out on the middle dock and looked back at the parking lot. According to the story, Becca'd arrived in a cloud of dust, leaped from her car, and dashed to the foundation's boat. As she pulled away from the slip, her perfect hair streaming, Agatha Anne had arrived and joined Bubo, who was yelling ineffectually at Becca to return. Less than a minute later, the boat had exploded.

I went to the covered dock, where I assumed the slips were rented on a permanent basis. From where I stood, the door of the office was approximately forty feet away. The door itself was open, but a warped and rusty screen door obscured the interior. It was not inconceivable that Becca's arrival had gone unnoticed until the moment when the boat's engine roared. The noise would have drowned out any voices, and with her back to the marina, she would not have seen anyone waving.

Wondering what disturbed Captain Gannet about the scenario, I went to the screen door and entered a large room with a few tables and chairs, a rack with postcards, a humming soda machine, open-topped coolers, and a counter laden with paraphernalia crucial to the gentle art of jerking fish out of the water by snagging their lips with metal barbs. Photographs of sportive souls who had experienced success in such humanitarian pursuits were thumbtacked to the walls amid curling yellow newspaper clippings and anti-quated license plates. A crudely printed sign announced the winners of a bass tournament from two years in the past. Perchance this year's would feature sopranos.

A man came through a doorway covered with what appeared to be a threadbare bedspread. He was in his twenties, with untrimmed but well-lubricated black hair, a thin nose, and the squinty eyes of someone who has at least momentarily contemplated a career as a serial killer. The sleeves of his blue cotton shirt had been chopped off to expose an amateurish tattoo on his spindly arm, and his jeans hung precariously on his gaunt hips.

He flashed tobacco-stained teeth at me. "Help you out?" he drawled in a tone that insinuated he was referring to my clothes. He emphasized the message by licking his lips and gazing at my admittedly svelte body.

"No, I'm just browsing. Are you the owner?"

"I suppose you can say I'm the manager, but it's a stretch. You interested in those fillet knives? That stainless-steel number on the far left can slice open a fish's belly in no time flat. You just poke the tip in and let 'er rip."

"I don't think so," I said, swallowing as I tried not to envision the technique. I went to the soda machine and fumbled in my purse for quarters.

"My treat," Bubo said over my shoulder, enveloping me in a sour odor as he put coins in the slot. "What's your preference?"

I wanted to mention a particular brand of deodorant, but randomly punched a button and grabbed the can when it rattled into the tray. I sat down in the nearest chair, hoping he could not sense my apprehension. I wasn't afraid of him. He was thin to the point of emaciation and had the pasty, porous skin and reddish eyes of a heavy drinker. Then again, I had no desire to find myself in a shoving match with someone less congenial than a junkyard dog.

He leaned against the machine, his pelvis thrust forward and his fingers kneading his thighs. "Funny place to browse."

"Well, I'm thinking about buying a house out here, and I wanted to find out what's available."

"I'm available most every evening after nine. My name's Bubo Limpkin. Yours is . . . ?"

"Not important," I said with a chuckle that may have sounded a bit manic (or similar to that of a chuck-will's-widow). "You don't seem to have many customers, Bubo. I'm surprised you're not busier on a Saturday morning."

"The real fishermen are already out on the lake. The college kids start showing up later in the morning, some of 'em already drunk. God, I hate those rich, snotty brats."

"What about the people who have lake houses? Do they use their boats on a regular basis?" I pointed toward the covered dock. "Is that where they keep their boats?"

"Some of them." He went behind the counter, disappeared briefly, and emerged with a can of beer. "Hate to let the damn frat boys get too much of a head start," he said as he popped the top and grinned at me. "Want one?"

"No, thank you. I believe we were discussing the homeowners. Is that far dock where they keep their boats?"

"Like I said, some of them. Right now I don't got any more slips to rent, but if you ask me sweetly, I might be persuaded to reserve one for you. What kind of boat are you thinking about? Party barge—or one with a snug cabin?"

I pretended to consider his question for a moment. "I might enjoy a cabin cruiser, but I've heard they can be dangerous because of the potential for fuel leaks. Wasn't there an accident in this very area a few months ago that involved propane?"

"Yeah, but it was a fluke. Those boats are as safe as a bedroom. I sleep in the back room, myself. It's fixed up real nice. Wanna see it?"

At this rate, Caron and Inez would have time to locate and identify all eight thousand species of birds, return to the lodge to pack, and be halfway to the highway before I gleaned one fragment of enlightenment. Furthermore, it seemed possible that sooner or later I would find myself in hand-to-hand combat with dear Bubo Limpkin if I allowed him to continue to manipulate the conversation. I opted for a Machiavellian tactic.

"I can tell you're on to me, Bubo," I said admiringly. "Okay, I'm not a potential buyer. I'm an undercover insurance investigator. We're not satisfied with the accident report, and before we pay the claim, we want to reexamine the facts."

"Suit yourself," he mumbled as he took a fillet knife from the counter and pulled it out of its leather casing. He slid the blade across his thumb. "This is one sharp mama, this one. You know, I don't recollect ever hearing of an undercover insurance agent. All the ones I've met can't wait to shake my hand and tuck a business card in my pocket. Why would you be undercover?"

"Think of me as a private investigator," I said as I forced my gaze away from the knife blade. "If you'll just run through what happened on the day of the accident, you can get back to work and I can head for the office."

"I ain't gonna talk about it."

"Maybe not to the press, but why not to me? I'm just doing my job, as were you the day of the accident. From what I've been told, Agatha Anne Gallinago reported a suspicious odor in the cabin that morning and asked you to check it. Late that afternoon, Becca Cissel arrived to take the boat, and you were out on the dock when the boat exploded. Is that right?"

"Close enough." He crumpled the empty can and tossed it into an overflowing plastic garbage sack. "Look, lady, I don't get paid to stand around and gab about what happened three months ago. I got things to do, so why don't you finish your soda and get the hell out of here?"

"Did Captain Gannet order you not to discuss it?"

"I don't take orders from him or anybody else. I got my own reasons for not talking about it, and plenty of them. You think I like this pissant job and a pissant salary that ain't enough to keep a body in beer and chaw? A week from now I'll be in Las Vegas, drinking champagne while a sweet little thing gives me a massage right down to the tips of my toes. If you want, we can go in the back and see how it feels. If not, scram."

"Is someone paying you not to talk about the accident?"

He came around the end of the counter, the knife in his hand, and started toward me. I decided it might be prudent to continue our chat at a later date, put down the can, and strode briskly across the room. No knife embedded itself in my back as I banged open the screen door, but I could feel a distinct tingle between my shoulder blades.

Once outside, I paused to wipe a sheen of perspiration off my forehead, then walked back to the dock where the residents' boats gently rocked. There was a fishiness to the air, not unsurprisingly, and a noticeable smell of gasoline. As I continued to the end, I spotted several dead fish drifting nearby, their eyes rounded with disbelief at their demise. The surface of the water was oily and littered with oddments of plastic and sodden paper. Lakes, I decided, were best appreciated from a civilized distance. Like Farberville, for instance.

I retraced my steps and was starting for my car when I heard Bubo's voice from inside the office. I eased to the edge of the screen door.

"She says she's an insurance investigator," he snarled, "but I don't care if she's from the FBI.

The ante has gone up and I want the money tonight." After a lull, he added, "That's what I
said—tonight. If you don't show up by ten, I'm
gonna start giving out interviews to anybody
with a checkbook!"

A telephone receiver was replaced with super-
fluous vigor. I hurried around the corner of the
building and crashed into a motionless figure.
He caught my arm to steady me, then released
me and stepped back to regard me with a smirky
smile. Between gasps, I reciprocated as best I
could. He was at least sixty, with an egg-shaped
head above broad, dandruff-spotted shoulders
and a much broader paunch. His hair was wiry
and peppered with gray, his skin mottled with
freckles and warts. He wore a frayed suit, a white
shirt, and a tie that would not have sold at a garage sale. And I had a really good theory as to his
identity.

"I've heard all about you, Mrs. Malloy," he
said in a voice as smirky as his expression. "Now
I have the honor of meeting you in person to
find out if your reputation is deserved."

"How do you know who I am?" I said coolly.

"Last night I just happened to drive by my
friend Dick Cissel's house and saw an unfamiliar
car. I'm curious by nature, always have been, so I
ran the plate this morning and made some calls. I
learned all sorts of things about you, your daughter, your duplex, your bookstore—and your reputation. You are a busy little snoop, aren't you?"

"You people who live out here need to find another topic of conversation, Captain Gannet. I'd suggest the national deficit or the environment, for starters, and then maybe the civil wars in Eastern Europe. I'm flattered that everyone seems so intrigued by me, but it's beginning to get on my nerves."

"Heard about your mouth, too," he said as he took a cigarette from his pocket and lit it, then blew a stream of smoke into my fuce.

My eyes stung, but I refused to blink. "I can't begin to convey how much I've enjoyed this, but I must be on my way."

He stepped in front of me. "Not just yet, Mrs. Malloy. I need to make something clear. You may have a free rein in Farberville on account of your boyfriend in the CID, but that doesn't wash in this county. You just get in your car and go on home, and don't come back until the eagles do. Most years that'd be December."

I was so stunned that I was at a loss for a response. At last I found my voice, stepped back only far enough to escape his foul breath and smoky emanations, and said, "I will not be bullied, Captain Gannet. I came to visit friends, and I shall return whenever I desire. I have no interest in what washes in this county. Apparently some of the residents do not on a regular basis."

"Your friend Dick Cissel might have trouble washing the bloodstains off his hands." He moved out of my path and gestured for me to go past him. "Drive home carefully, Mrs. Malloy, and watch for deer in the road. A couple of kids hit a buck last year, and their car flipped into a tree. One of them had a broken neck, the other two broken legs and a ruptured spleen."

"Thank you for your concern." I stalked around him, got in my car, and left him in a rain of gravel and a cloud of dust. I turned on the first road I came to, then pulled over and cut off the engine to allow myself to regain control of my temper. I'd heard blunter lectures from Peter concerning my involvement in criminal matters, but he was always polite about it. Gannet was lucky I had not given in to the impulse to kick him in the shin. I rather wished he'd accosted me on the end of the dock—and subsequently found himself treading water with dead fish.

I still had several hours to kill before I went back to Dunling Lodge. I'd worn out my welcome at the marina, alas, and I'd not noticed a mall in the vicinity where I could idle away the time. I did have a book in my overnight bag (the motto of a dedicated mystery reader: be prepared), so I decided to find a picnic area and amuse myself in an uneventful fashion.

The road proved to be a dead end. Sighing, I turned around and tried again, being careful to avoid the road to the marina. I mentally replayed the conversation with Bubo. He'd implied he was blackmailing someone, and his remarks on the telephone seemed to confirm it. Had he noticed someone tampering with the boat? Rather than responding to Agatha Anne's directive to check for a fuel leak, had he approached the guilty party and agreed on a price? If so, he would be an accessory to premeditated murder and hardly inclined to give interviews. Had Captain Gannet been the least bit gracious, I would have told him about the call I'd overheard seconds before we collided. As it was, I wouldn't have told him about a meteor plummeting toward his head.

I narrowly avoided a pickup truck filled with screaming children and grim parents, and seconds later, another dragging a boat on a trailer. Picnic areas seemed noticeably lacking, or cleverly hidden. I realized I was approaching Dunling Lodge and kept my eyes on the road as I passed the top of the driveway. I was definitely going in circles, which was not catastrophic, but at some point I would run out of gas. The Rover was not parked in front of Dick's house.

Grumbling to myself, I tried another road, this one deeply rutted and cluttered with loose rocks and beer cans. At the bottom of the hill was a trailer. It was sadly neglected and unkempt, bleached with age, surrounded by waist-high weeds and the skeletal shells of unidentifiable appliances. Behind the trailer were obscure structures of splintery boards, tin, and chicken wire.

As I eased over a particularly treacherous rut, a man came from behind the trailer and yelled, "Hello! Can you be doing me a favor?"

I braked and looked at him. He was very blond, very tan, very tall. His legs were long and muscular, as were his arms, and he moved with the grace of a gymnast. He wore a tight T-shirt that emphasized his chest and shoulder muscles, and little bitty shorts that emphasized other muscles best left unspecified. As he came to the edge of the road, I got a better look at his deep blue eyes and lopsided smile. He had a charmingly boyish face, but at this distance I put his age at forty.

"I did not mean to alarm you," he continued in a lilting Nordic accent. "It is only that my truck will not start and I am needing a ride to Dunling Lodge. I am Anders Hammerqvist."

"Claire Malloy," I said weakly.

"Luanne's friend, yes? She has told me all about you. You lead a most exciting life, from what I have heard."

My personal incarnate of Boswell could save time if she wrote my biography and distributed a copy to everyone who came to Turnstone Lake. "Don't you operate a facility for wounded birds?" I said.

"Yes, that is exactly what I do. Would you like to investigate it, too?"

"Too?"

"Luanne says that you are here to help Dick clear his name. He is a kind man who would never hurt anyone. You can park here and I will show you what birds are now in my care. Last week I had three hawks and a barn owl, but yesterday two of the hawks were able to be released. I also have a litter of rabbits and a rattlesnake that was run over in the road. In the winter I often have eagles as my guests. They are my favorites."

I parked the car and got out. "Did you rescue an eagle the day of Becca's accident?"

"No," he said, his affable smile replaced with an odd look. "Agatha Anne told me that Becca had been told of an injured eagle on Little Pine Island. A deputy and I took my boat and went there, but I was not seeing an eagle. This was strange, was it not?"

6

As we went around the corner of the trailer, we were greeted by a piercing scream. I grabbed Anders's arm. "What was that?" I managed to whisper despite the sudden dryness of my mouth.

"One of my guests," he said, covering my hand with his and squeezing it. "He is easily startled. The owl will also hiss or scream at you if you get too near. I do not need a watchdog with these two around."

I warily admired the red-tailed hawk, while he regarded me through the wiring with immeasurable malevolence. Anders proudly showed me fresh scars on his wrists from attempts to coax the bird onto a heavy leather glove. The idea struck me as masochistic. The hawk was almost two feet high from head to tip, and its beak curled downward at an ideal angle to rip flesh. It appeared eager to do so at any time, including the present. As we stood there, the holes in the chicken wire seemed to grow larger, the wire itself thinner, and the plywood less firmly secured.

"Will you release it soon?" I asked.

"No, I am sorry to say. He has a damaged wing that will be keeping him from flying ever again. When he is healthy, officers from the park service will take him to schools to teach the children. It is sad that he must remain in captivity, is it not?"

I could almost feel talons digging into my skin, but I nodded sympathetically and allowed myself to be shown a gold-and-brown owl that obligingly rotated its heart-shaped face to stare at me. We moved on to a straw-lined box filled with hairless creatures that Anders assured me were baby rabbits. After I'd declined to examine the recuperating rattlesnake, I agreed to a glass of vodka before returning to Dunling Lodge, telling myself I was doing so only in order to ask him about Becca's accident. His wonderfully exotic accent played no factor in my decision, nor did his shorts.

The living room of the trailer was clean and minimally furnished with a sofa, a rickety maple chair, and several well-stocked bookcases. On the walls hung photographs of birds and a large surveyor's map of Turnstone Lake. The windows lacked curtains, but it was hardly the neighborhood to worry about voyeurs. Through a doorway I caught a glimpse of an unmade bed. A voice in the darkest corner of my mind mentioned that it was king-sized and the sheets appeared to be satin. Sternly reminding myself of my virtuous motive, I refused to listen further.

I sat on the edge of the sofa and accepted a small glass filled with a clear liquid. "*Skoal*," I said as I took a cautious sip. Midmorning was a bit early for undiluted alcohol, but I was a sleuth, not a sissy.

"*Skoal*," Anders said, downing his in a gulp. "So, why are you driving down here this morning, Claire?"

The truth seemed silly, so I opted for evasion. "Agatha Anne told me about your facility. You were living here before the Dunlings bought the lodge?"

"For twenty-one years. I like people well enough, but I am more happy with the company of birds and animals. They are more trustworthy." He refilled his glass and sat down at the far end of the sofa, crossing his very long legs and giving me a beguiling smile that sent fine lines radiating from the corners of his mouth and eyes. "I am from Malmö, a big city with too much pollution, too many people, too much traffic, too expensive. Turnstone Lake is quiet, with not so many people. Here I can do as I wish, which is to doctor animals during the day and drink vodka and party with my friends in the evening."

"Did you come to the United States on a student visa?"

"A long time ago, yes. Now you should be

telling me about your investigation, Claire. What have you discovered?"

I noticed his smile was forced despite the determined twinkle in his eyes, which was likely to be reflexive from all those years of squinting into the midnight sun. "Mostly that Captain Gannet is a jerk," I said lightly. "I gather that everyone else out here is friendly. Did you know Becca well?"

"She was breathtakingly beautiful, vivacious, as eager as a schoolgirl to learn. Many days she came here to help me feed the animals and clean the cages. At first she was afraid to go near the big birds, but she became less nervous after a time and more admiring of them. One afternoon I found her crying because one of the eagles had died. She had a tender heart."

We were back to the increasingly stale theme of her perfection, I thought somewhat testily, waiting for him to describe her halo and wings. "Had she been here the day of the accident?" I asked.

"She may have come by that morning; about that I am not sure. At noon I drove into town to pick up supplies, and when I returned, Agatha Anne and Georgiana were here. When they realized it was getting late, they left together. An hour later, Agatha Anne returned to tell me the terrible news about the explosion." He paused to stare at the floor, his blond hair flopping into his eyes as he shook his head. "I felt very bad, of course. Becca was an angel."

I winced only slightly. "So I've been told. Were you at the party when she threw the quiche?"

He went to the kitchenette and refilled his glass. His back to me, he said, "Yes, we were all at Dunling Lodge when she and Dick had a small argument. It meant nothing. Everyone had been drinking steadily, as happens when the weather is cold and we are inside too much." He returned and sat beside me, his thigh brushing mine, his expression intensely earnest. Anticipating a bombshell, I was disappointed when he tossed out an insignificant firecracker. "They were in a corner, whispering to each other. Dick's face was red, and Becca looked as if she might be soon crying. Abruptly he walked away. She lost her composure and . . ."

"Nailed him," I said. "Then you don't know the cause of the argument, Anders? She never gave you any hint that there were marital problems?"

"Dick worshiped her, as all of us did." He rose unsteadily and picked up my empty glass. "Can we now be going to Dunling Lodge? I have no telephone, and I need to call the veterinary supplier about a drug shipment that has not yet arrived. It is not so long a walk, but I would prefer to ride with a beautiful woman such as yourself."

I managed not to simper, although I may have come dangerously close to it. Some men emit an undercurrent of sensuality, but Anders was an electrical storm. Ozone filled the cramped confines of the trailer. I doubted I was the only woman who'd felt the urge to fling herself into his arms and allow sweet Swedish nothings to be whispered in her ear. Out of what was surely misguided loyalty to a certain cop, I restrained myself and tried to think how to approach a possible variation on that scenario with delicacy, if not diplomacy.

"So Becca came here often?" I said as we went to my car. "In the mornings or afternoons?"

"Whenever she could." Anders held my elbow as we stepped over the ditch at the edge of the road, then released me and folded himself into the car. "She was very interested in the birds."

And perhaps the bees, I added to myself. I turned around (one of my principal activities at the lake) and we headed for Dunling Lodge. "Do you have any ideas why Captain Gannet continues to investigate the accident?" I asked casually, watching him as best I could as we bounced from rock to rut.

"Well, as I was telling you, we found no eagle on the island. Captain Gannet questioned me many times about that, but all I could tell him was that it was not there when his deputy and I searched for it. It may have recovered, or it may have been attacked by a larger predator. The raptors have no aversion to cannibalism. Also, everyone who was known to have been on the lake that afternoon was questioned by Captain Gannet himself, but no one admitted to calling the office. It is rare that we receive anonymous calls of this nature. Most people are aware of the law and are indignant when it is broken. The bald eagle is your national symbol, is it not? Even hunters can be patriots when they think they may receive a reward."

"But Agatha Anne had a message from Becca on her answering machine. That's why she went to the dock, isn't it?"

"This is what Agatha Anne has told Captain Gannet many times." He then inadvertently risked our lives by putting his hand on my leg and murmuring, "Will you be staying at Dick's house tonight? I could not visit last night, but if you are there, we will drink vodka and watch the stars appear. You can see many more stars here than in town."

I gripped the steering wheel and ignored certain shrill biological imperatives. "No, I'm going back to Farberville at noon. My daughter and her friend are training to be facilitators, and I promised them I'd wait until they returned from a bird walk. They're . . . not sure they want to continue."

I parked beside the Jaguar, which was pristine despite the dusty roads. It did not look as if it ever tolerated a single mote of dust, much less mud splatters or avian offerings from above. My car looked as if it needed to be sand-blasted. Anders and I went around the side of the house, passing by the garden behind formidable fortifications, and onto the patio. Neither Dunling was there, although the bird feeders were doing a brisk business and the lake was buzzing with boats.

Anders put his arm around me and squeezed my shoulder. "Are you sure you cannot stay tonight, Claire? I can take you on an owl prowl. We will take only a small flashlight and a blanket, and walk far into the woods, where it is very private and the moon shines through the trees with a silvery light. If we do not at first see an owl—well, we will find ways to amuse ourselves while we wait."

"I have to go back," I said resolutely. "Now I'd better find out if the girls have returned from their hike. Don't you need to make a telephone call?"

The back door opened and Caron strolled onto the patio, a pair of binoculars dangling from a strap around her neck. Her nose was sunburned and her bare legs covered with scratches, but she looked surprisingly cheerful.

"We got back an hour ago," she announced, critically eyeing Anders and then me to make sure we were not on the verge of engaging in unseemly behavior (as defined by Mr. Lawrence). "We saw like fifty different birds, or at least Agatha Anne did. She kept pointing and whispering about four o'clock in the oak and three in the pine. Inez and I squealed a lot and pretended we were looking at something more fascinating than foliage."

Inez eased out behind her. "There weren't any

snakes, Mrs. Malloy. Caron screamed once, but it was just a lizard in some dry leaves."

"And you didn't leap onto my back?" Caron retorted without mercy. "I felt like Quasimodo's twin sister."

I introduced them to Anders. They responded politely, but I could see they were more interested in scanning the lake for barges than in making polite conversation with a venerable Viking. Anders excused himself and went inside to use the telephone.

"You seem in good spirits," I began with due circumspection.

Caron was much too engrossed in a methodical sweep of the lake to lower the binoculars. "We're done with the dumb stuff. After lunch, we get to learn to drive the barge. Next weekend we have to wear dorky official shirts and caps, but today we can wear our bathing suits. Tomorrow we're supposed to familiarize ourselves with the office procedures and do really, really challenging things like answer the telephone and put out brochures, and if our handwriting is deemed acceptable, address invitations to some fund-raiser—" She broke off with a gasp and began to fiddle with the focusing knob.

Inez made a futile try for the binoculars, shrugged, and sat down on the bench. "So we agreed to stay," she said.

"Then I'm off," I said to her and to Caron's back, refusing to allow myself to speculate about an owl prowl. Peter and I had an understanding, even if neither of us understood it very well—and it was more a source of migraines than moonlight. Until it was resolved, I could not with a clear conscience embark into the woods or anyplace else with a flashlight and a blanket. Anders had invited me to nothing more emotionally significant than a dalliance. Well, an exceedingly romantic dalliance. Twenty years ago I would have been packing a picnic basket with a bottle of wine and a loaf of bread, but I was now an adult with mature and carefully cultivated expectations from relationships. I just wasn't sure what they were.

"Why are you still standing there?" Caron asked, albeit with minimal interest. "I thought you said you were off. I'd like to think you weren't referring to your rocker, but from the way you were panting after that hairy old guy . . ."

"I'll see you two tomorrow," I said. I went into Dunling Lodge and down the hall to the office to tell Agatha Anne that I was leaving. If Anders was still there, I would smile warmly in order to ease the disappointment that I was certain would engulf him with the intensity of Bubo's miasma. I was so caught up in my compassion that I ignored a flurry of giggles and opened the door. And stopped in the doorway.

Agatha Anne's face was rosy as she wiggled out of Anders's arms. "Claire, what a surprise. I thought you'd already gone back to town."

"I'm leaving now," I said, admittedly disgruntled to discover how fickle his affections were. "The girls seem eager to finish their training, and I have a bookstore to run. Luanne will bring them home tomorrow when you're done with them."

"They're fast learners," she said, still flustered, still rosy, still looking at me as if she wished she had an automatic weapon in her designer pocket. "About what you saw, Claire . . . Anders and I were talking about poor Becca, and I was overcome with sadness. He was comforting me."

Anders nodded obediently. "It is hard on Agatha Anne when she remembers the tragedy."

Laughing ruefully, she moved behind the desk and began to rearrange pieces of paper and manila folders. "Thank you so much for bringing the girls, Claire. Do you need directions back to the highway?"

I shook my head and left the office. Obviously Anders took care of more than birds and bunnies, I thought as I went across the living room to the front door. I reached for the knob, then stopped as a gunshot resounded like a clap of thunder. After the echoes faded, I opened the door guardedly. Birds were flapping away in all directions, their squawks more annoyed than alarmed.

Wharton Dunling stood at the corner of the house, his face shaded by a broad-brimmed straw hat. Smoke curled from a cigar clenched between his teeth as he studied the edge of the woods adjoining the garden. "I got you this time, you miserable hairball!" he chortled, the cigar bobbling with each word. Negligently swinging the shotgun in one hand, he went to the first line of defense and beamed at the rows of leafy green.

"Hello," I called as I approached him. He was as intimidating as a swarthy bandito, and the last thing I wanted to do was startle him. If he felt remorse for his recent kill, he was disguising it well. "I'm Claire Malloy, Caron's mother."

"What those girls need," he said without looking at me, "is a dose of boot camp. Six weeks in a sweltering wasteland would stop all their whining and complaining. They'd be damn grateful for a glass of tomato juice." On that charitable note, he walked around the edge of the concertina wire, muttering under his breath, and continued to the edge of the woods. He squatted next to a hole near a log, found a stick, and began to jab at the opening. "Crawled off to die, did you?"

I could think of no reason to prolong the encounter, and was about to get into my car when he stood up and said, "You're the woman who's investigating the boat accident, aren't you?"

"I brought Caron and Inez up here yesterday," I said, "and I'm on my way home right now. I apologize if they've failed to express their gratitude for your hospitality. It's a symptom of their age, I'm afraid." I reached once again for the car door handle.

"Wait," he commanded in a voice that must

have unnerved many a boot camp trainee. He threw down the stick and strode across the parking lot, his face still shadowed by the hat and his eyes nearly invisible. Cigar ashes wafted behind him like light snow. "I heard you were asking questions down at the marina earlier this morning. Did that scum Limpkin tell you anything?"

"He refused to discuss the accident. He told me to scram, but that's about all."

Wharton halted on the opposite side of my car. "What about Gannet? What'd he have to say?"

"Pretty much the same thing," I said. "Is there something one of them should have told me?"

He cackled unpleasantly. "I suppose Bubo could have told you that the accident was caused by his negligence, but he's not the type to accept responsibility. As for Gannet, he reminds me of a sergeant I knew over in Korea. I was a lieutenant fresh out of OTC, and he was a grizzled twenty-year man who'd finally figured out that he wasn't going to make general before he retired. He took it hard."

"And?" I murmured, wondering if I was to hear something significant.

"And he went for a walk in a minefield." He cackled more loudly. Flecks of spittle sizzled on the roof of my car. "Gannet needs to watch his step. The Dunling Foundation means everything to my wife. Ten years ago she inherited a lot of money from some uncle out in California. Neither of us cares about fancy possessions, and we sure as hell had our fill of travel, courtesy of the United States Army. Instead of saving it so it could go to distant cousins, Livia decided to fund a foundation that will have a lasting impact on the environment. Anyone who attacks its reputation is going to deal with me first."

"Gannet seems to think this was the finale of a marital dispute. Nobody's implied that the Dunling Foundation's reputation is involved."

"The boat belonged to the foundation, and some sleazy lawyer might take it into his head to persuade one of the gal's relatives to file a lawsuit. Dick's a good man, and he's assured me he won't, but lawyers can smell a potential suit like a hyena can a hunk of rotting flesh. We carry some liability insurance because of the barge excursions. It's not enough to cover a million-dollar judgment against us." He fitted a shell into the shotgun and pointed it at the groundhog's burrow. "Considering how fond Gannet is of poking around, it's a damn shame he can't poke out his head."

I decided it was time to leave before he realized that I'd been invited to prove the accident was the fault of none other than the Dunling Foundation. As Agatha Anne had said, it would not be wise to wiggle my nose and whistle at the moment. She'd been joking, but Wharton Dunling was hardly smiling.

I glanced in the rearview mirror as I started up the driveway. Livia Wharton stood in the doorway, watching me. She looked no more congenial

than her husband, and there was no vagueness in
her frown.

After I'd consulted the map and memorized
the necessary turns, I headed for the highway, doing my best to concentrate on the immediate goal
of making it back to Farberville without further
delays. And went slower and slower, and finally
pulled to the side of the road and stopped to consider what I'd heard from various people. There
were incongruities and inconsistencies. The only
point of convergence seemed to be Becca's perfection, and I was beginning to wonder about that.

And whom had Bubo Limpkin called? It had
been around nine o'clock when I'd left the marina office, walked out on the dock, and returned
to eavesdrop. Gannet had been outside seconds
later, so he was not the recipient. Anders had said
he didn't have a phone. Supposedly Agatha Anne
was blazing a trail through the woods with two
surly campers wagging their tails behind her, but I
didn't know what time they'd left Dunling Lodge.
I didn't know where Georgiana, Sid, Wharton,
and Livia had been—or, for that matter, Dick,
Luanne, and Jillian. It was logical to assume that
some of the above could provide alibis for others
of the above. For all I knew, they all could have
been attending a lecture on my previous cases.

And it could have been someone whom I'd not
yet met, which wasn't at all sporting. Or I could
have misunderstood Bubo, who was far from the
epitome of articulateness. I'd assumed he was

making a blackmail demand, but he could have been talking to his stockbroker. If he'd seen me walking toward the office, he could have been talking to a dial tone simply to entertain himself at my expense. Why he would find it entertaining was a little hard to explain, but so was more and more of what was happening at Turnstone Lake.

Reminding myself that only a few hours earlier I'd been grousing about the impossibility of proving Becca's death had been accidental, I ordered myself to resume driving. Yes, Luanne was my best friend and her happiness was important to me. Yes, Gannet had aroused in me what might be best described as a mildly competitive spirit. Proving him wrong would be satisfying.

The obvious thing to do was to tell him about Bubo's mysterious phone call, then return home and perhaps even call Peter Rosen to inquire politely about his itinerary. I reminded myself of my selfless gesture made on his behalf. Becca Cissel was not the only candidate for sainthood. My sacrifice was not the sort one could crow from the roof of the portico, obviously, and I would never acknowledge my momentary indecision to anyone, including Luanne.

I pulled into the gravel lot of a convenience store and filled my tank with what must have been a vastly superior brand of gasoline, considering its exorbitant price. No one with a house at the lake fretted over nickels and dimes; this was the burden of the middle class. My theory was reinforced as I went inside and noted the prices of staples such as bread and milk. Hoping the pay telephone in the corner did not require a gold card, I offered a fistful of dollars for the gas and accepted a handful of change.

I was looking up the number of the sheriff's department when a man came into the store. He related what must have been an off-color joke to the proprietress, who blushed and said, "Scottie Gordon, when are you gonna grow up? I swear, my ten-year-old grandson tells the same jokes and laughs as hard as you do."

The name was familiar. I looked over the edge of the telephone directory at the man, who was tall and mildly heavy, with a neatly trimmed beard and the amiable demeanor of a teddy bear. He turned to study the shelf of chips with the seriousness of a battlefield general. Scottie and Marilyn Gordon were the couple who had introduced Becca into the group. Had they met her at Mother Teresa's house while she was hanging halos out to dry?

I decided to ask, although not with that precise phrasing. Scottie was gnawing his lip and sighing as I came down the aisle. "I'm Claire Malloy, a friend of Dick Cissel's," I began timidly.

"Hey, I've heard of you," he said, or rather, boomed. "Agatha Anne was telling Marilyn and me all about your successful investigations. So, how's the case coming? Found any Maltese ducks among the mallards?"

I solemnly vowed that if by some inexplicable and unimaginable twist of fate I became a legitimate celebrity, I would swim out to sea until I encountered a shark with an attitude. "Not yet," I said. "There's something I'd like to ask you, though. It's not all that important, but if you have a minute . . . ?"

"Sure, if you'll come back to the house with me. Marilyn would kill me if she found out I met you and she didn't get the chance. It's not more than a mile from here. You can follow me, and then interrogate us on the deck over a Bloody Mary."

Or I could get in my car and follow the highway home in time to open the store for the waning hours of the afternoon. "Okay," I said.

The Gordons' house looked familiar, which meant only that I'd driven past it in one of my haphazard attempts to find something else. I was ushered inside and introduced to Marilyn Gordon, who did not appear to harbor any latent tendencies for spousecide. She was attractive in an anemic way, with soft brown hair and sad eyes. We went to the deck and settled on redwood chairs. Moments later, Scottie appeared with a pitcher and glasses.

"I wanted to ask you about Becca," I said before he could demand the details of my earlier involvements. "I understand that she first came to Turnstone Lake to visit you. Was she an old friend?"

"That bitch?" gasped Marilyn. She clapped her hand to her mouth and stared at me as the word hung in the air.

I sat back and smiled, confident that I'd finally come to the right place.

7

"Now, Marilyn," Scottie said as he came over to squeeze her hand, his forehead creased and his voice reproachful, "the poor girl's dead. There's no reason to carry a grudge for what happened a long time ago, and we may have misunderstood her motives."

She wiped her eyes on a cocktail napkin, tossed back her drink much as Anders had done with the vodka, and made a face as the black pepper and Tabasco caught up with her. "I apologize," she said to me. "I shouldn't have said what I did. Everyone else adored her, and it's inappropriate for me to speak ill of her. This is my third Bloody Mary of the morning; otherwise I wouldn't have been so vulgar."

I was not interested in postmortem proprieties, but I decided to tiptoe around the subject for the time being. "When Becca first came to Turnstone Lake, she was visiting you, wasn't she? But she wasn't an old friend?"

"Hardly," said Marilyn, making a similar face for what I presumed was an entirely different reason. "Three years ago I went to Miami to move my mother into a nursing home. It was stressful for both of us, and I was thoroughly numb and exhausted when I arrived at the airport. My suitcases were so heavy that I could barely drag them to the counter, then all of a sudden this beautiful young woman was carrying them for me and making sure they were properly tagged. It turned out we were on the same flight. Once I'd checked my luggage, she invited me to join her for coffee. I noticed some bruises on her face that she'd tried to cover with makeup. She admitted that two weeks earlier she'd been brutally mugged and had ended up with bruises, broken ribs, a staggering hospital bill, and no job. I tried to buy her dinner, but she refused. After a great deal of protesting, she agreed to accept a hundred-dollar loan. Only later did I realize how gullible I'd been, but it was too late."

"You were being kind," Scottie said in a tone that implied he'd said the same thing many times. "She took advantage of you, that's all."

"Oh?" I said, trying not to salivate too openly.

Marilyn sighed. "She did it well, too. When our flight was called, Becca helped me with my carry-on bag, found me a pillow and a blanket, and persuaded the woman in the seat beside me to trade with her. She asked about my mother, and listened with great sympathy as I described the ordeal. She absolutely insisted that I have several drinks to calm my nerves and bought them herself despite my misgivings."

"You were weaving when you came off the plane," Scottie said with a grin, "and hiccuping most enchantingly."

She managed a rueful laugh, but then gave him a penetrating look that made it obvious she did not share his nostalgia. "Becca had to carry my things and steer me to the gate. Once she'd handed me over to Scottie, she asked if we could recommend an inexpensive motel. I found myself insisting that she stay with us, and after a display of reluctance, she agreed. She was an ideal houseguest, although I was a less than ideal hostess. I was so drained from the week in Florida that I could barely find the energy to get dressed in the morning or get through the afternoon without a nap. I seemed to misplace my reading glasses and car keys every time I set them down, and on two occasions I forgot to turn off a burner on the stove. Becca was terribly sweet and understanding. She cooked and cleaned, walked the dog, retreated to her room every evening to allow us privacy, and bought me little gifts to cheer me up. She even sent cute cards to my mother. It seemed rude to ask her when she was leaving."

"Did she say why she was coming to Farberville?" I asked.

Scottie shook his head. "Not really, just that she was afraid to live in Miami any longer. She was adept at steering the conversation away from herself. Frankly, it was flattering to be met at the door with a martini and breathless demands to hear about my day at the accounting firm. When our daughter was that age, she was too preoccupied with her own social life to do any more than wave as she sailed out the door."

"When our daughter was that age, she was married with a baby and a full-time job," Marilyn corrected him tartly. "Becca may have looked and behaved like a college girl, but she was closer to thirty than twenty. The dresser in the guest room was littered with bottles of skin lotion, cleansers, mud packs, and the like, and it took her an hour to put on makeup in the morning. You were too busy sucking in your stomach to look carefully at her."

I did not want the illuminating conversation to degenerate into marital mayhem. "She never made contact with anyone in Farberville?"

Marilyn stopped glaring at Scottie long enough to say, "I don't think so, Claire. I never heard her talking to anyone on the telephone, and the only times she left the house alone were to run errands for me or to walk the dog."

"I asked her almost daily if she was bored," added Scottie, "but she just referred sadly to her emotional trauma. She wasn't exactly receptive to hints."

Marilyn rolled her eyes. "I did everything short of packing her suitcase, but I was reared to be a gracious hostess to the bitter end. Finally, Scottie and I told her we were going to spend six weeks here at the lake, and that she would find the group much older and their conversations tedious. We've stopped going to the parties ourselves because we simply do not share their enthusiasm for birds."

She shrugged at her husband, who picked up the narrative. "Becca was sitting in the backseat of the car before I'd finished loading it. She'd bought some bird books at a used-bookstore and was studying them as if she anticipated a final exam. She also asked about everyone in the Blackburn Creek area until I felt as if I'd been through a session with the IRS." He took our empty glasses and went inside.

Marilyn waited until the door was closed. "I was too embarrassed to admit how foolishly I'd behaved, so I merely introduced her as a friend from Miami. The men immediately fell all over her, but she refused to flirt with any of them. I'd hoped that she and Anders would hit it off, but she made it clear that she wasn't interested in a romance with anyone—single or married. She never said or did one thing that warranted criticism. Scottie and I finally threw up our hands and resigned ourselves to the situation. Pathetic, isn't it? We're in our fifties and we reared two children. Scottie has managed a large office for nearly thirty years, while I taught math to bored teenagers, some of whom are in prison by now.

And neither one of us could figure out how to rid ourselves of one young woman."

I said nothing, remembering the times I'd allowed people to take advantage of me. Caron was at the top of the list (with Luanne a close second), but I'd been seriously inconvenienced by a significant percentage of the population of Farberville. I could easily understand Marilyn's predicament. It came from the curse of being mild-mannered and amiable. Attila the Hun did not have this problem.

Scottie returned with replenished drinks and bowls of chips and peanuts. "The last time Marilyn drank on an empty stomach, we ended up with a houseguest for six months—and I did notice a suitcase in your car."

"Six months?" I said.

Marilyn nodded. "But only in a technical sense. At the end of July, we went back to Farberville. Becca asked if she could stay here. We readily agreed and were halfway home before we dared breathe—or look in the backseat to make sure she wasn't crouched on the floor. I felt obligated to call her every now and then, but she assured me that she wasn't the least bit lonely. I understood why when we received the marriage announcement in December."

I realized the afternoon was dwindling away as we gossiped, but it was refreshing to hear about the darker side of Miss Congeniality. I appeased my growling stomach with a few peanuts, then said, "Agatha Anne mentioned that Becca and Jan Cissel became close friends before the accident at the end of the summer."

"What a terrible thing that was," Marilyn said as she used a fresh napkin to wipe the corner of her eye. She went to the railing of the deck and bent her head for a moment, then turned around and tried to smile. "Jan was one of my dearest friends. She was involved with the bird group, but she loved to read biographies, and we'd sit out here and talk about them for hours. I think she was a little perplexed by Becca's attentions, but also flattered. Becca persuaded her to buy a new wardrobe and have her hair styled at a pricy salon. They went into Farberville several mornings a week for aerobics, lunch, and shopping."

Scottie made a noise not unlike that which came from my stomach. "You should have heard Dick when the credit card bills started coming. He grew up poor, and he and Jan scrimped for years while he was in dental school and training in his specialty. Once he and Sid got the practice established, he started doing well, but I've done his taxes for twenty years and he's had some lean times. He's not a miser, but he feels more comfortable knowing he has a safety net. Jan was ripping substantial holes in it."

I made a mental note to suggest to Luanne that she ask for an audit before she opted to become the third Mrs. Dick Cissel. I would have suggested autopsies, too, had they been possible.

He'd been devoted to his first wife, but also angry at her extravagance. He may not have been enchanted with Becca's extravagance either. Neither woman was shopping now.

"Has Captain Gannet talked to you?" I asked.

"Briefly," Marilyn said, "but as I mentioned, we rarely socialize anymore, and after the marriage, we had very few casual encounters with Becca and Dick. When did we last see them, Scottie?"

"At a Christmas party in town. Dick was looking miserable in a tuxedo, but so were most of the men. Becca had on a skimpy black dress. One of the waiters was trying so hard to peer into her cleavage that he fell in the fountain." He paused, and his cheeks began to glow as Santa's purportedly did when he chanced upon cookies and milk. "I play golf with Dick every once in a while. The last time we played was in the fall, and he asked me some questions about Becca's past. I felt like a real idiot when I didn't have any answers."

Nor did I. I did, however, have a final question of my own. "Did Becca borrow any more money from you during her stay?"

Marilyn looked at her husband, who shook his head emphatically. "Not a penny," she said. "I wondered about that myself. When we left the lake that summer, there were essentials in the cabinets and a few things in the freezer, but certainly not enough to keep her going for what turned out to be nearly four months. I never quite found the nerve to ask her if she was receiving regular checks from a trust fund or an annuity of some sort. I wish I had."

Scottie had been glancing surreptitiously at his watch, and now he and his wife exchanged uneasy looks. I thanked them for the drink and went to my car, all the while trying to assimilate this new version of Becca as a parasite with more tenacity than mistletoe.

It was past three o'clock. By the time I drove to Farberville and threw open the doors of the Book Depot, the pedestrians would be home preparing for the interminable merriment of a Saturday night in a college town. This was not to imply that I could not telephone Gannet from the convenience store, go home, and spend a peaceful evening with the newspaper and a novel. The next morning I would hear of Bubo's attempt at blackmail and the identity of his victim. If instead I was regaled with the details of Luanne's untimely demise at the hands of her lover, I would spend the rest of my life ravaged by guilt. It was a most annoying dilemma.

I turned back toward the lake.

Assorted cars were parked at Dick's house, including the Jaguar and the Range Rover. I knocked on the door, waited, and finally went inside. As I hesitated at the edge of the living room, Jillian came out of the kitchen with a tray of sandwiches.

"You're back," she said. "Luanne said you'd gone home."

Her voice expressed neither pleasure nor disappointment, although I would have put my money on the latter. I opted to interpret it as a statement of fact. "Oh, but I didn't. It's so beautiful up here that I couldn't drag myself away to Farberville. Is Luanne here?"

She gestured for me to follow her to the deck, where I found myself interrupting that which I dread worse than root canals and quarterly tax estimates—a meeting. Clues abounded. Agatha Anne had a clipboard in her lap. Georgiana Strix had a notebook in one hand and a pen in the other. Livia Wharton was peering doubtfully at an engraved invitation.

Only Luanne was unarmed, but she had the look of an animal with its leg in a steel trap. She jumped up and came to grab my arm before I could retreat. "I'm so glad you're here, Claire! Let me get you some iced tea. Would you like me to fix you a plate of sandwiches and cookies?"

I lowered my voice to a snarl. "I would like you to unhand me. You know how I am about clipboards."

Agatha Anne gave me a bright smile. "Please join us, Claire. We're trying to finalize the details of the Rapturous Raptors Ball, and we'd truly appreciate your suggestions."

Georgiana smiled wanly. "Please do."

I was pushed firmly onto a settee beside Agatha Anne. "Where are the girls?" I asked her.

"Out on the barge, familiarizing themselves

with some of the islands and coves. They have a map." She perused the top page on the clipboard and sighed. "Becca was in charge of the arrangements with the hotel, the caterer, the florist, and the band. I can't tell what deposits have been made, but I can find out on Monday."

"What if she didn't make any?" asked Georgiana. "Last year the caterer wanted five thousand dollars in advance. What will we do?"

Livia put aside the invitation. "We'll write them a check, of course. There should be plenty of money in the account to cover trivial amounts like that. We raised over two hundred thousand dollars last year. Surely some of it went into a reserve fund?"

"Well, yes." Agatha Anne pretended to write something, but I caught a glimpse of a series of squiggles along the margin before she flipped the page. "But I hate to dip into the reserve. The claims adjuster says we should receive a settlement for the boat within a week. It might be better to use that."

Livia clucked disapprovingly. "I don't see why. The Dunling Foundation cannot risk its reputation. Our funding depends on the generosity of the community, and if we are perceived to be careless or even the tiniest bit irregular in our financial dealings, donations will dry up. If the caterer does not have a deposit, he should be sent one as soon as possible. The hotel will not keep the ballroom open indefinitely, and the orchestra may well accept another engagement. Agatha Anne, will you please make the necessary calls Monday morning? If deposits are needed, Georgiana can put the checks in the mail immediately."

Georgiana's face seemed to shrink into her frizzy hair, and her voice drifted out in a thin whine. "I'm still trying to straighten out the books, Livia. Becca adopted a system that's awfully complicated, and I'm having trouble with it. The Dunling Foundation doesn't want to start bouncing checks with the local merchants."

"I should say not!"

Agatha Anne leaned forward to pat the older woman's knee. "Please don't worry, Livia. Georgiana and I will work on the books all weekend. It's really just a matter of reconciling the balances of the checking accounts, the money market account, and the various treasury bills and bonds with last year's expenditures. We'll start as soon as we're finished here."

I raised my hand. "Why was Becca doing the books?"

Georgiana's eyes began to glitter. "She took over for me when Barry left. I was too distracted by lawyers and hearings to do a proper job, and just looking at all the invoices and statements and canceled checks was enough to . . . make me want to kill myself!" Sobbing, she ran down the steps and around the corner of the house. Seconds later we heard a car drive across the rocks.

Agatha Anne rose hastily. "Meeting adjourned.

Livia, we'll be at the office in an hour or so and get to work. Luanne, hang on to that list of likely donors for the silent auction, and sometime tomorrow we'll discuss how best to approach them. Perhaps Claire will help you." She fluttered her clipboard in farewell, then hurried after Georgiana.

"Ah, well," Livia said as she stood up, her hand clutching the armrest of the chair to steady herself, "I suppose I'll wander on now. Wharton will be wanting a martini before long, and I'm not at all sure I have any olives. Do you think he'd notice if I tucked a piece of pimento in a grape?"

Luanne diplomatically aimed her at the sliding glass door. "There are at least three jars of olives in the refrigerator. Please take one with you."

They went inside. I assumed I was alone, and therefore was startled when Jillian said, "Livia's like a mockingbird, isn't she? She can change her tune to fit any occasion. Feeble old woman with a heart condition, or shrewd old autocrat— whatever's expedient. Georgiana's more of a one-note singer."

I jerked my head around and saw her in the shadows at the far end of the deck. "I didn't intend to break up the meeting," I said, perhaps mendaciously, "but it does seem curious that Becca was acting as bookkeeper. Did she ever mention having experience in that field?"

"She managed a chic dress shop in Miami, and I think she said something about doing those books. People underestimated her mind because she was so beautiful, but she was very clever. I saw that the first time I met her."

Luanne came back outside and collapsed into a chair. "I'm not sure how I ended up with the list of donors. I loathe wheedling, and I'm not chummy with all these bank presidents and CEOs. Last year Becca talked them out of several hundred thousand dollars' worth of goodies." She ran her fingers through her hair, sighed, and looked at me out of the corner of her eye, "Maybe a tag-team approach would be best. One of us could present the information about the Dunling Foundation's good deeds, then—"

"Forget it," I said. "Where's Dick?"

Luanne opened her mouth, but Jillian cut her off, saying, "He took the boat to go fish by the dam. He said it was his only hope of avoiding Captain Gannet for a few hours. I'm going to run into town to get a newspaper, wine, and some steaks for dinner. Father has yet to catch a fish. If he ever does, he will have invested several thousand dollars in it. It should be tasty."

After she left, I told Luanne what I'd learned from the Gordons. She listened and nodded right up until I suggested that Dick might have had a motive to do away with his wife.

"You're wrong," she said as she went down the steps and disappeared around the corner of the house.

"Maybe," I said to no one but myself, having

finally managed to clear the deck, in a manner of speaking. I took a book from my purse, propped my feet on the table, and settled back to spend a pleasant afternoon. The only interruption was a blast from a shotgun, indicating that Wharton's earlier chortle of triumph had been overly optimistic.

No one had returned by nine. I stood in the kitchen and ate a square of cold lasagna, then carefully rinsed off my plate and put it in the dishwasher. I considered leaving a note, but if Dick was planning to deliver a payoff to the marina at ten o'clock, I had no desire to advertise my presence.

The front right tire of my car was flat. I was not too much of a feminist to accept a manly hand with the lug nuts, but there was no hand in the vicinity. I popped the hatch and started to work.

It was dark by the time I parked on the road above the marina and walked down the eroded road. A lone utility pole cast a weak light on the parking lot and the back of the building. The only vehicle in the lot was a pickup truck, the words "Blackburn Creek Marina" painted on the door. Across the back window was a gun rack, and on the bumper an oblong sticker extolling the virtues of fishing over our cherished Puritan work ethic.

Since this was my first time to attend such an affair, I had no idea of the protocol. Would the victim creep through the woods—or would he (only in the generic sense; I am a firm supporter of equal rights) drive up, toss a bag out the car window, and demand a receipt? In either case, my presence would not be appreciated. I edged around the lot and eased into the heavy shadows next to the office. Light spilled out of the doorway, but I could see no sign of Bubo in the front room. I needed a safer place from which to observe the transaction, I decided as I contemplated the limited possibilities.

Earlier I'd had a clear view of the door from the dock. I tiptoed around the oblong of light and headed for the row of expensive toys. Feeling like a trespasser, I stepped onto a party barge and found a reasonably comfortable spot to sit between two mounted chairs. If someone were to come searching with a flashlight, I would be found within seconds, but I doubted Bubo and his guest would care to prolong their encounter.

My adrenaline began to ebb as I sat and waited, wishing Bubo had been thoughtful enough to provide me with a more precise time. The barge rocked gently, and its creaking was almost soporific. A light breeze had blown away most of the gasoline fumes, and the fishiness seemed less pronounced. In the woods, birds chirped and screeched, and I heard a peculiar call that surely came from a chuck-will's-widow. Low male laughter drifted across the water. I finally saw a boat several hundred yards away; its occupants appeared to be fishing rather than engaging in an illicit rendezvous.

The office remained empty. No light shone through the bedspread that covered the entrance to the back room, but Bubo's truck was in the lot. My only hope was that he was waiting in the dark, busily planning how to spend his windfall.

It's possible that I lapsed into a fantasy about an owl prowl. I was no more familiar with its protocol than I was with that of blackmail, although I had some rather steamy theories. I squeezed my eyes closed and tried to insert an image of Peter's face into the scenario, but it refused to come into focus. Sighing, I leaned against one of the chairs and rested my head on its plastic cushion.

The sound of a boat's engine roused me from a convoluted dream dominated by hawkish glowers (Peter's) and spiraling cries (Caron's). I raised myself to my knees and saw that the fishermen had decided to move on to what they must have felt was a more fertile spot. Dreams are unreliable indicators of the passage of time, and I had no idea how long I'd dozed.

I usually kept a small flashlight in my purse, but I'd locked it in the car and brought only my key. Having breached marine etiquette by trespassing, I decided snooping hardly counted. In a blessedly unlocked compartment I found a flashlight and briefly shone it on my watch. It was well after eleven, which meant I'd slept for at least half an hour. Nothing had changed inside the office; the front room was empty and the back room unlit, so it was likely that I had not missed anything of significance.

I stood up and stretched, replaced the flashlight, and stepped off the barge. As I glanced at the lake, I saw a bobbly light on the far shore. I continued to the end of the dock. Perhaps Anders had persuaded someone else to prowl for owls, I thought wryly, and they were seeking the ideal spot to spread a blanket.

I was speculating on the identity of the distaff owl prowler when something slammed into my back and I went flying off the dock. Spread-eagle, I might add.

8

I hit the surface with a splash—and a gasped expletive—loud enough to be heard across the lake, or even in the next county. My arms flailing, I plunged downward. The coldness of the water did little to encourage a careful analysis of the situation, but it did shock me into action. I floundered to the surface, swallowing several gallons of Turnstone Lake in the process, and managed to suck in a breath before I shoved dribbling hair out of my eyes and glared up at the dock. Whoever shoved me had not lingered to learn if swimming was among my multitudinous talents. Guarding the flank was not, obviously.

"Thanks a lot," I grumbled as I treaded water. This current dilemma was more than annoying—it was downright infuriating. There was no ladder conveniently situated nearby, and it did not seem likely that my assailant had rushed away to find a life preserver or a pole. It occurred to me that said assailant might have gone to fetch a gun to finish me off. A few cautious movements brought me under the dock, where ribbons of light shone through the planks and glittered on the oily water. I listened for footsteps above my head, but I heard only the creaking of the boats and the blithe chirping of the damn birds. My arms and legs were growing less responsive. If I kicked off my shoes, I would be obliged to walk barefoot across the parking lot and up the road to my car—presuming I did not succumb to hypothermia. Or to a bullet in the forehead.

I couldn't continue to tread water much longer, but there was nothing to cling to under the dock. As I eyed the slimy pilings, something stroked the back of my neck. I clamped my hand on my mouth to hold back a screech, and tried very hard not to think about snakes or eels or carnivorous catfish or anything else more diabolic than a branch floating in the water. This was not as easy as it would have been were I sitting on my sofa in the middle of a sunny afternoon.

Whatever it was touched my neck again, this time with increased pressure. I turned slowly and saw a hand. It seemed reasonable to keep my own on my mouth for the moment, although small noises were escaping. The hand was white, and its only motion—the rippling of splayed fingers—came from the waves I was generating. It was attached to an arm, which in turn was attached to an oddly bloated torso. The head hung below the water. As I stared, bubbles streamed from beneath it and it began to sink into the blackness.

It was time to Get Out Of The Water (in Caron's vernacular). If my assailant was waiting to shoot me, he or she was welcome to try. I swam out from under the dock and headed toward the boat ramp, unable to stop myself from imagining the hand reaching for my leg, clamping itself around my ankle, dragging me back to a cold, watery grave. I realized I was whimpering in a most undignified fashion, but I couldn't stop myself. My arm hit a submerged stick; my subsequent gurgle was distinctly undignified. I spat out a mouthful of water and paddled more frantically. As soon as I felt rocks beneath me, I found my footing and charged up the ramp with the fury of a Rough Rider. The parking lot looked the same. Bubo's truck was still parked beneath the utility light. I had a reasonable idea of his whereabouts, but it was not the moment to confirm my hypothesis.

Alternately cursing and shuddering, I started for the road where I'd left my car, then stopped in the middle of the lot and forced myself to reconsider. There was a telephone in the office. In the time it would take to drive to Dick's house and call the sheriff's office, the corpse might drift out into the lake. The water was cold enough to retard decomposition for weeks, if not longer, and the body would not rise to the surface until sufficient gases formed within the tissue. I'd never seen what the police call a "floater," but I suspected it was not a pretty sight. The ensuing investigation would be hampered by the nibbling of fish.

I crept down the dock and peeked through the screen door. Nothing appeared to have been disturbed, and if my assailant was inside, he or she was either crouched behind the counter or waiting in the unlit back room. I licked my numb lips, then eased open the door, not at all confident that I'd made an astute decision.

"Hello," I called. "Is anybody here?"

If I'd received an affirmative answer (or even a negative one), I would have been one very unhappy bookseller. All I heard was a distant whippoorwill. Exhaling in relief, I went behind the counter and dialed 911. This resulted in a mechanical voice informing me that my call could not be completed unless I first dialed a one. I dialed a zero instead, and told the operator to connect me with the sheriff's office. The shrillness with which I did so was effective. A disconcerted deputy promised to send a car as soon as possible, and I reluctantly agreed to wait in the office.

After I'd hung up, I realized my teeth were chattering. Icy trickles from my hair ran down my face and back. My clothes clung to me as if they'd been dipped in glue rather than water; my shoes sloshed with every step. I eyed the bedspread that hung in the doorway of the back room. Peter Rosen had been heard to make acerbic comments about civilians who'd tampered with the scene of a crime, but the only crime I could be sure of had taken place at the end of the dock. The medical examiner would be the one to determine if the corpse under the dock had died of unnatural causes.

I yanked down the bedspread. There was no yelp of surprise or muffled gasp from within the dark room. Once I'd removed my shoes and draped myself in a makeshift sari, I felt for a light switch and turned on what proved to be a bare bulb in the middle of the ceiling. It was obvious that Bubo's bedroom had been searched. Even the sloppiest housekeepers prefer their mattresses on the bed, their drawers in the bureau, their bowling trophies in some semblance of order. A pillow had been slit, and everything in the room was dusted with tiny white feathers. A framed photograph of Bubo and a dead fish lay on the floor, the glass shattered. Pockets had been ripped off an army surplus jacket. A tackle box lay upturned, and hooks and lures were scattered on the stained linoleum floor.

"What are you dressed up for—an orgy?"

I spun around and blinked at the figure silhouetted behind the screen door. The stooped shoulders and smirky voice were both familiar. "That was quick, Captain Gannet," I said levelly.

He came inside and sat down next to one of the round tables as if he were going to have a late supper. If he'd pulled out his handkerchief and tucked it under his chin, I would have burst out laughing—despite the fact I was wet, cold, and had been swimming with a corpse. As it was, only a slightly hysterical giggle escaped, I bit my lip and waited.

"What was quick, Mrs. Malloy?" he said as he took out a crumpled pack of cigarettes and placed it in the middle of the table in lieu of a more elegant centerpiece. "Surely you're not referring to my wit?"

"Not at all. I called the sheriff's office no more than three minutes ago. The adolescent who took my call said it might take as much as ten or fifteen minutes to get an officer here."

"You and Bubo in the mood for three-way sex? You're not too bad for a middle-aged broad, even with your hair plastered down like that, but as for Bubo—well, he's just not my type."

All of the potential responses that flashed through my mind were apt to land me in a jail cell. I settled for a humorless chuckle, then said, "I called the sheriff's office because of the dead body under the dock. If you've finished making ribald remarks, you might want to see if it's still there. I didn't see a face, but Bubo's truck is here and he's not. Furthermore, his room is in noticeable disarray. I'm just a middle-aged broad having a bad hair night, but I would suggest that someone searched it."

He did not take this well. His face turned the color of raw beef and his eyes bulged. Spittle formed in the corner of his mouth, and I could tell

he was on the verge of a major exhibition of outrage. I was a little disappointed when headlights
flashed on the dock and car doors slammed.

"Goodness, we have company," I said as I
sailed out the door to greet the troops.

The ensuing hours did not sail by. A deputy
gave me a thermos of coffee, then stationed himself by the door. Men huddled on the dock, con-
versing in low voices and barking orders in loud
ones. The sheriff himself arrived, and after I'd
talked to him, I found myself longing for Gannet's smirk and dandruff-coated shoulders. Flash-
lights competed with headlights. Car radios
crackled. The back room was photographed
and some of the more promising objects were
examined for fingerprints. Despite my repeated
avowals that I had not stepped foot in the room
or touched anything except the telephone, I was
deemed as promising as a bowling trophy. I
cleaned my fingers on the bedspread.

Two divers in shiny black wet suits worked off
a barge, and at dawn they brought up the body.
It was Bubo, to no one's surprise. Gannet identified him, the coroner pronounced him dead, and
the ambulance crew zipped him up in a plastic
bag and took him away. The sheriff conferred
with Gannet and left, as did the coroner, whose
pajama cuffs were visible around his ankles.

Only then did Gannet come into the office,
kick out a chair, drop his bulk into it, and rub
his red-lined eyes. His lower face was gray with

emerging whiskers, and I suspected his breath had not improved after many hours of cigarettes and coffee.

"Let's go through it one more time, Mrs. Malloy," he said wearily. "Yesterday morning you overheard Bubo threaten someone on the phone. You kept it to yourself, naturally, because you fancy yourself to be a hotshot amateur sleuth. You came back here at ten o'clock to find out the identity of the blackmail victim. Either Bubo was already dead or you were asleep at the critical moment."

"If there was a critical moment," I said. "Isn't it likely that Bubo was killed by some redneck looking for money?"

"Even rednecks are wily enough to open the cash register. The money's still there. Bubo was infamous for begging for credit at the bars by the middle of the month. The only things anybody'd expect to find in his bedroom are fleas and used condoms."

"Then Bubo got drunk and walked off the edge of the dock."

"We haven't ruled out anything. There's a contusion on the back of his head, so he could have knocked himself unconscious on one of the boats as he fell. The boys'll start looking for smears of blood when it gets lighter. It's a real shame you won't be able to enjoy the sunshine from your cell."

"What's the charge?" I countered. Even though my hair and clothes were dry, I began to shiver. I'd done time in the Farberville jail. Okay, I'd been out within half an hour—but the experience had not been agreeable and I'd refused to accept my mug shot as a souvenir. "Is it against the law in this county to swim after midnight?"

"Save your smart remarks for your boyfriend on the Farberville police force. Around here, we prosecute folks for interfering in an investigation. You should have told me what you heard, and until you come up with an acceptable explanation why you didn't, you can sit in a cell."

I gave him a facetiously surprised look. "I have an explanation, Captain Gannet. You're a bully and a pig. I don't like you."

He took his cigarettes from his shirt pocket and hunted through his other pockets for a lighter. Or for handcuffs, I thought uneasily as I watched him. He finally found a book of matches, and once he'd lit a cigarette, said, "So now you got all the answers. That's just great, Mrs. Malloy. Here's another question for you—where is Dick Cissel's boat? I happen to know he rents a slip out there, but at the moment it's as empty as a dead man's eyes. When you surfaced from your little swim, did you hear a boat leaving the marina?"

"No, I did not," I said, refraining from mentioning the boat that had awakened me. It had left several minutes *before* what Gannet condescendingly had described as my "little swim." "Why are you so quick to assume Dick had anything to do with this?"

He regarded me through a swirl of smoke, his mouth puckered and his eyes thoughtful. "Well, it's like this. If he arranged the so-called accident that killed his wife, then he's the logical candidate for blackmail. He may have decided it was cheaper to bash Bubo on the back of his head and leave him floating beside the dock than to pay him off. We redneck cops are always sniffing around for motive and opportunity, and Dick Cissel has both. Where's his boat?"

"Jillian mentioned that he'd gone fishing, which I gather is one of the more conventional activities at a lake. There's no evidence that he arranged anything. Agatha Anne reported the propane leak that morning, and no one could have predicted that Becca would take out the boat before the leak was repaired. Dick wasn't even at his lake house that day."

"How insightful, Mrs. Malloy." Gannet rocked back and folded his arms across his broad belly. "However, he was seen at this marina the night before, long after he claimed to have gone back to Farberville. His Range Rover was parked up the hill where your car is right now."

"Seen by whom?"

"Seen by a witness with no reason to lie. Cissel, on the other hand, has plenty of reasons to lie. I checked his long-distance bill for the day of the accident. He made a short call from his home in Farberville to his lake house. The so-called accident happened half an hour later, which I estimate is long enough for his wife to call the Gallinago house and leave a message on the answering machine, drive here, and take off for the island to save an injured eagle. Problem is, the Swedish vet and one of my deputies went out there and found nothing. The report was a fake. It was made to get Becca Cissel on that boat."

I thought about it for a minute. "How could the caller know that Becca wouldn't get hold of anyone else? If Agatha Anne or Georgiana had been home, one of them could have been on the boat with Becca."

"Maybe he didn't care, Mrs. Malloy. I need to go home and shave before I get down to business. I'll allow you to go to Cissel's house if you promise to stay there until I say otherwise."

I assured him that I would and exited before he changed his petty, dictatorial mind. My car was as I'd left it, although the windshield had been graced with a white blemish. The culprit had flown, but its parting gift seemed an appropriate summation of the night.

I found my way back to the house with only a few false turns. In that it was not yet seven o'clock, I tapped softly on the front door. When no one appeared, I determined that it was locked and went around to the deck. The sliding glass doors were also locked. I lay down on the wicker settee and put my arm across my eyes, wishing I'd brought the ink-stained bedspread with me. Despite the frenetic twittering of birds and the distant sounds of truly dedicated fishermen, I fell asleep.

"Claire? What on earth are you doing out there?"

I opened one eye and squinted at Luanne, who stood in the doorway with a cup of coffee. Her hair and makeup were immaculate. She wore a silky peignoir and matching slippers, as if she anticipated being swept into a musical comedy. I opened the other eye and determined that the sun was significantly higher. "Sleeping," I said crossly. "Is there cream in that coffee?"

"What happened to your hair?"

I sat up and tried to salvage my comely red curls. The movement sent barbs of pain to my neck, which had been forced into an unnatural angle due to the limitations of the settee. When you, Dick, and Jillian failed to return last night, I went for a swim at the marina."

"You did what?"

She was in the mood for questions, but I'd already had my quota for the day. I went to the kitchen, poured myself a mug of coffee, and returned to the deck. Before she could resume her interrogation, I related the events of the night, omitting particulars of the final conversation with Gannet. "He's liable to show up anytime," I added, "and he'll want to know where everyone was from sunset until midnight."

Luanne tried to laugh, but the result had a strangled edge. "We certainly weren't at the Black-burn Creek Marina. I walked down to Anders's trailer. We talked about eagles until it grew dark, then he drove me back. I assumed you'd gone to Farberville. Jillian called to say she'd decided to stay in town."

"What about Dick? Did he fish all night?"

"He was in a remote cove when the boat's motor conked out. He paddled to a marina, but it was closed and everyone gone. He had to walk for hours down back roads until he found a house where the occupants were awake and willing to let him make a phone call. He called me about eleven-thirty and I picked him up half an hour later."

"Gannet's going to love the lack of alibis," I said as I finished the coffee and put down the mug.

"Why do we need alibis? Did Gannet say something you didn't tell me? Did he accuse Dick of this—this thing?"

Honesty is critical to friendship, but not necessarily indispensable. "No, not really," I murmured, "but he has questions." I went to the rail and looked across the cove at Dunling Lodge. Its mistress was sharing the picnic table with various birds and squirrels—and her binoculars were aimed squarely at me. I waved, then dropped my hand as I remembered the rippling white fingers under the dock. "I wonder how the girls are doing. I don't see them on the patio."

"I'm sure they're fine," Luanne said coldly. "I wish you'd be honest with me, Claire. If Gannet's determined to link Dick with Bubo's accident, he must have said something."

"Bubo's accident?" Dick said as he came out the doorway with a plate of pastries and a pot of coffee. "What happened?"

Between bites, I again related the story, then stopped to think over what I'd said. "Bubo must have been dead when I arrived. He could have fallen off the dock, or he could have been hit on the head and encouraged to fall. In either case, the splash would have awakened me. But someone was there more than an hour later."

"Impressive reasoning," Gannet said from the bottom of the steps. "I didn't mean to eavesdrop, but I couldn't help myself when I heard the dulcet tones of Mrs. Malloy here. I'm beginning to think her reputation is deserved." He came onto the deck, dressed in a fresh shirt and a jacket already dotted with ashes and flakes. I noted with a flicker of pleasure that his eyes were still red and he'd nicked his chin while shaving. "I had a word with the medical examiner at the hospital in Farberville," he continued. "Normally the body sinks right after death, but Bubo was wearing a nylon jacket that trapped enough air to keep him afloat right up until Mrs. Malloy disturbed the water. But it couldn't have kept him up very long."

"Then why didn't I hear a splash?" I said.

Gannet shrugged. "Guess there wasn't one. We found an empty whiskey bottle over by the boat ramp. There wasn't any blood on it, but there weren't any fingerprints, either. We're wondering if someone used the bottle to bash Bubo, eased him into the water, and then washed it and put it down real quietly so as not to bother Mrs. Malloy while she was taking herself a nice little nap." He bared his teeth at Luanne and Dick, who were as motionless as salt and pepper shakers. "Now, if you two would be so kind as to tell me where you were last night . . . ?"

I went inside to take a scalding shower and change into clean shorts and a T-shirt. I then polished off another square of cold lasagna, and was conscientiously rinsing the plate when Luanne came into the kitchen.

"That dreadful man!" she said as she snatched the plate from me and jammed it into the dishwasher. Glasses and silverware clinked nervously.

"Shall I assume you're referring to Gannet?"

"Of course I am! He made Dick go with him to the other marina to verify that there's something wrong with the boat. He said there was plenty of time for Dick to have gone to the Blackburn Creek Marina to murder Bubo and then return to the other marina and hike up the road to call me."

I stepped out of her way as she began to pace, grumbling and reeling about like a windup toy. The kitchen was large enough to accommodate such activity; if she'd tried it in my kitchen, she would have imperiled her toes. "Gannet does seem bent on proving Dick is guilty of something," I said as I retreated behind the breakfast bar.

"Or me! He pointed out that I was alone last night. Dick almost punched him in the nose, but he just said that I could have done it. He's not all that convinced that you didn't do it."

"Me? Oh, that makes a lot of sense. I killed Bubo and shoved his body into the water, then threw myself off the dock so that I could discover the body and report it to the authorities."

Luanne paused in midstep. "That's a fairly accurate synopsis of what he said."

"Why stop there? Why not accuse us all of conspiracy? What about Agatha Anne and Georgiana? The Dunlings? Why leave out the Gordons and the lecherous vet?" I threw up my hands and forced Luanne to retreat as I commanded the track. "And the entire membership of the Audubon Society! Maybe Bubo was shooting partridges in pear trees. Livia Dunling called the national headquarters and they sent out a murder of crows! In that case, the coroner will be dealing with 'caws' of death!"

"What is wrong with you?" Caron said from the doorway. "Are you doing this menopause thing again?"

Luanne hustled her into the living room before I could leap across the breakfast bar. "Your mother has been accused of murder, Caron, and she's not handling it well," I heard her say in a voice that was not entirely sympathetic.

"Who's she accused of murdering?" Caron asked in a voice that was not entirely incredulous, for that matter. "Anybody I know?"

I followed them into the room. "Probably, since you and Inez took out the barge yesterday. My purported victim is the man who ran the marina."

"Oh, him. He leered at us just like the chemistry teacher started doing before they took him away in an unmarked van." Having dismissed my heinous crime, she turned to more important matters. "Is there anything to eat around here? We had fish and canned peas for dinner last night and bran for breakfast. I'm so dizzy I barely made it here." She emphasized her condition by collapsing on the sofa and sighing plaintively. "My stomach stopped growling ages ago. I think it's devouring itself out of starvation."

Luanne offered to make a sandwich and went into the kitchen. Considering the contents of the refrigerator, it was likely to be made with pâté rather than peanut butter. I sat down and steeled myself for another outburst if Caron was confronted with liver.

"Where's Inez?" I asked.

"Addressing envelopes. If she keeps at it, she should be done in six or eight hours."

"Why aren't you doing the same thing?"

She raised her head to give me an injured look. "Agatha Anne said my handwriting was too sloppy for her expensive envelopes. I was supposed to file a bunch of stuff, but I decided to take a break and root for truffles. There weren't any alongside the road."

"You have attractive handwriting," I said sternly.

"Not in this weakened state," she said as her head fell back and she closed her eyes. "I could barely dot the i's, much less cross the t's. Inez may appear wimpy, but she has a much stronger constitution. She was scribbling her heart out when I stumbled out of the office."

She was more likely to have slithered out a window when Inez wasn't looking, but for some inexplicable reason, I was reluctant to launch into a lecture about betraying one's best friend. "Were you and Inez in the office last night?" I asked.

"Yeah, for a couple of hours. Agatha Anne and Georgiana had all these checkbooks and ledgers spread out all over everything. They kept spouting off numbers until I thought I'd go mad. As long as they have enough money to pay me next weekend, they can pretend to be vice-presidents of the Chase Manhattan Bank all they want—and as long as I don't have to be there. Inez and I sat on the floor in a corner and sorted millions of stupid brochures. All of a sudden Georgiana started crying. Agatha Anne told us to beat it."

"In those exact words?"

"No, Mother. She told us we were excused for the rest of the evening and we needed to work on our owls. The only thing I'd like to do to an owl is stuff it. Don't you think a great horned owl would look nifty on the mantel? Better yet, I could hold it up in Rhonda Maguire's bedroom window and hoot. Supposedly they go *hoo, hoo-hoo, HOO HOO*. Rhonda would wet her pants!"

Luanne looked a little bewildered as she returned. "What was that supposed to be—an ocean liner?" she said as she set a plate on the coffee table.

Caron suspiciously lifted the top slice of bread. "What's this?"

I grabbed my purse and hurried out the front door, although not in time to avoid hearing a horrified voice say, "Goose liver?"

I drove up to the road and stopped, since I had no destination in mind. Captain Gannet had ordered me to stay at the house until he gave me permission to leave, but he was at the far end of the lake. It was tempting to go to Farberville. I would be brought back in handcuffs and leg irons, however, and not even Peter could save me. Not that he would necessarily try, I thought with a twinge of remorse for my arch refusal to consider the cruise. He'd probably been sitting home in front of the television, watching a dreary baseball game and eating cold pizza at the precise time I'd been fantasizing about Anders Hammerqvist.

I drove to the convenience store and went inside to call Farberville's Finest and apologize. Obliquely, of course, but with great sincerity. After digging out all my change, I called Peter's house. He answered on what would have been the last ring had he not picked up the receiver.

"Hello," I began, intending to ease into the apology when it seemed suitable.

"Oh, Claire," he said, breathlessly rather than delightedly. "What's up?"

"Am I interrupting something?"

There was a pause. "Well, I guess you are. I invited some of the guys from the department to play touch football and cook hamburgers. I called you Friday evening, all day yesterday, and a couple of times this morning. Where are you?"

In the background I heard outbursts of laughter and bantering. Not all of "the guys" had gruff, masculine voices; some of them were sopranos. I explained that I'd come to the lake on Friday, intending to return home the following morning. I was about to elaborate on the cause of the delay when one of the sopranos called, "Come on, Rosen! It's first and ten, and you're the quarterback!"

Instead of mentioning the murder, I said, "Don't let me keep you from your guests."

"No, that's okay. So why didn't you come home yesterday morning? Did Caron and Inez get carried away by an eagle?"

"I believe it was a great horned owl. I'll tell

you about the rest of it when I get back." I hung up the receiver and ordered myself not to envision Peter's teammates, one of whom surely looked like a distaff version of Anders—right down to the little bitty shorts. It was possible Peter and I had been fantasizing about the same thing at the same time.

I bought a can of soda and was sitting in my car, staring bleakly at the windshield, when Sid Gallinago pulled up beside me.

"Hey, Claire," he said, "what're you doing?"

I doubted he wanted to hear the ugly truth, so rather than announce that I was in the throes of petulance, I said, "I came to get a soda."

"I heard about your adventures last night. If Agatha Anne had been the one to find the body, she'd still be squealing like a stuck pig. She can play rough when it comes to protecting her damn birds, but she sure as hell couldn't have handled that."

It occurred to me that Agatha Anne was at the Dunling Foundation office and I was in the presence of the person who best knew Dick Cissel. I smiled modestly. "We do what we must. I'm surprised you're not on the golf course today, Sid. Sunday afternoon, not too hot, blue sky."

"I played eighteen this morning," he said, mimicking my modest smile. "You want to come over and have a drink?"

"What a wonderful idea," I said.

His smile vanished and he gave me a somber

look. "Thanks, Claire. There's something I want to discuss with you. I'm really worried about Dick, but not the same way Agatha Anne and the others are. I'm starting to wonder if he really is implicated in Becca's death."

9

The Gallinagos' house, like the Gordons', was familiar, but only because I'd driven down the road on several occasions. The house was built with the same materials as most of the others: native rock, redwood, and glass. I parked and followed Sid inside. The living-room decor was a profusive jumble of corals and fuchsias and other subtle designer colors with exotic names. It was the perfect roost for Agatha Anne, who undoubtedly had a closet filled with clothes chosen to coordinate with the upholstery.

I opted for iced tea. Sid supplied it, as well as a beer for himself, then sat across from me. "I've known Dick for thirty years. We were roommates at the Kappa Sig house all through school. Opening a practice together seemed natural, even though Dick had to twist my arm to get me to specialize in pedodontics. We got married the same year, bought houses in the same neighborhood, and joined the same country club when the practice began to thrive."

"And later bought lake houses only a few miles apart. Do your boats match?"

"We don't go around town holding hands," he said, giving me a narrow look. "Dick plays a lot of tennis and racquetball; I play golf every spare moment. Agatha Anne and Jan were friendly, but Jan was a little too shy to keep up with the country club matrons and their incessant golf and tennis tournaments, charity affairs, luncheons, and so on. She always looked uncomfortable at cocktail parties. We used to tease her about the number of times she called home to speak to the babysitter." He put down his drink and rose. "Let me see if I can find something," he said as he left the room. A minute later he returned with a framed photograph and handed it to me. "This is of the four of us on a vacation in St. Croix about ten years ago."

They were standing in front of a row of bright flowers, with palm trees towering behind them. Jan was attractive in a puppyish way, with cropped dark hair, a large and noticeably sunburned nose, and a strained smile. Her sundress emphasized her thick waist and freckled arms. Sunglasses hid her eyes, but I had an idea they would have been lowered. Sid wore a gaudy shirt, Bermuda shorts, and sandals. He held up a drink festooned with fruit and a pink paper umbrella; his grin was lopsided and his eyes unfocused. Dick and Agatha Anne could have graced the cover of

People magazine, all tanned and sleek, toasting the camera with glasses of champagne. He wore white shorts and a shirt emblazoned with an animal. Agatha Anne's starchy white tennis dress brushed the top of her thighs, and a fuzzy yellow sweater hung around her shoulders. Her wristbands and socks were yellow. I wouldn't have been astounded to see a yellow tennis racquet in the background.

I studied Jan's expression for a minute, then handed back the photograph. "You look as though you were having fun," I said.

"Yeah, there's a great golf course down there, as long as you don't mind playing around the cows in the middle of the fairways. And watching your step."

I wasn't interested in the golf course or its pedestrian perils. "You said you wanted to talk about Dick, Sid. I can't stay too long. Captain Gannet may show up, and he won't be pleased to find me here."

"Because of what happened to Bubo Limpkin last night?"

I nodded. "Gannet's interested in everyone's whereabouts last night between sunset and midnight. I'm afraid it may be a formality. He seems to be concentrating on Dick—as usual." I paused delicately, but Sid failed to volunteer the pertinent information. "Someone mentioned that Agatha Anne and Georgiana were at the foundation office. Did they work all night?"

"I don't know what time they quit. I made my-self dinner, watched a couple of videocassettes, and went to bed at eleven or so. My golf date was at seven this morning. I wanted to be at my best so I could get back some of the money I lost last week. I ended up three over par, and it would have been two if I hadn't screwed up on seven-teen. That damn putt cost me fifty dollars."

"About Dick?" I persisted.

Sid pulled out a handkerchief and wiped his forehead. Looking unhappy, he said, "I don't know what Dick's told you, but there's a reason why Gannet keeps pestering Dick about Becca's accident. I keep telling Dick to be straight with Gannet. He won't do it, and sooner or later Gan-net's going to find some hard evidence and Dick will find himself facing a jury. You've dealt with this before, Claire. Lying to the police makes you look guilty as sin."

"Is that all Dick's guilty of—lying to the po-lice?"

He went from unhappy to utterly miserable. "I wish I knew. He's so damn stubborn that he won't even tell me what went on that night. Gan-net claims that Dick's Rover was parked near the marina, which means Dick could have gone down to the boat and loosened a fitting to create a slow leak. Dick insists he wasn't there, that he and his Rover were in Farberville."

"Gannet said he had a witness," I admitted. "He wouldn't say who it was, though."

"He hasn't told Dick, either. What I haven't told anyone until now is that I was worried about Dick after he stormed out of the party, announcing to one and all that he was returning to Farberville. He'd had several drinks and he stumbled over the mat as he left. When Agatha Anne and I got back here maybe an hour and a half later, I called to make sure he'd gotten home okay. Nobody answered. I tried again an hour later, and there was still no answer. I was damn glad to hear his voice the next morning."

"Did you ask him where he'd been the night before?"

"He said he was asleep and didn't hear the phone. Kind of hard to believe that, isn't it?"

"There are a lot of things that are hard to believe," I said under my breath, then added, "You saw Dick every day at the office and out here on weekends. Did you get the idea he and Becca were having marital problems?"

He went into the kitchen and returned with another beer. Resuming his seat, he said, "No, Dick never said anything to me. He's a great guy and my best friend, but we've never confided in each other the way women do. He's always been reserved, even back when we were chugging beer at the frat house and telling lies about the sorority girls. He was on scholarship. I used to wonder if that made him uncomfortable."

"What did you think about Becca?"

"She was a great gal," he said. "I dated a few

lookers in my day, and most of them were pretty damn snooty. Becca was a knockout, but she was more interested in the people around her than she was in checking her lipstick in the mirror. The first year they were married, she'd come by the office a couple of times a week with freshly baked cookies. She made sure all our staff received flowers on their birthdays. When our grandson was born, she sent him an antique silver christening cup and a teddy bear three times bigger than he was. When Agatha Anne's father passed away unexpectedly, Becca took charge of the telephone and flower deliveries and stuff like that. Afterward she helped Agatha Anne sort through her father's things and decide how to dispose of them."

I warned myself to keep a civil tongue, but a wee bit of irritation may have crept into my voice. "I've already heard how relentlessly perfect she was, Sid—but no one ever is. She was a mortal, just like the rest of us. The night before she died she was slinging quiche, for pity's sake. I'd make a lot more progress if one person would give me a realistic assessment of Becca. Do you know why she came to Turnstone Lake with the Gordons?"

"They said she was an old friend," he said uneasily, as if I'd dropped a labyrinthine essay question into the middle of a true-false test. "I seem to recall Agatha Anne saying that Marilyn was depressed about her mother's mental deterioration and was having a hard time coping, so Becca volunteered to stay and help out."

That was one interpretation, and certainly a popular one. Then again, Sid remained uneasy, which suited me fine. I sipped my drink and let him stew for a long moment, then said, "But you didn't believe she was quite so perfect, did you?"

"I'm a pedodontist, not a psychologist—but no, I didn't. She never once flirted with any of the men, or even gazed suggestively. As far as I know, Agatha Anne's faithful, but she can't control herself when she looks at the golf pro or even our own Anders. Georgiana's the same way. She can be sobbing about Barry one minute and panting over some virile young man the next. Becca acted like a virgin who'd been raised in a convent—voluntarily."

"So what did you think that indicated?"

"I never could decide if she was genuinely uninterested or if she was putting on an act. She must have known that all she had to do was wink and she could have had any man in the room."

"She didn't waste much time after Jan died," I pointed out politely. "She and Dick were married within a few months, weren't they?"

He started to speak, then closed his mouth and mulled over what amounted to an accusation. I suspected he'd been more intrigued with Becca's physical demeanor than with her behavior in matters that did not directly involve particular areas of his anatomy. Testosterone can have that impact on the male brain.

"Well," he said at last, clearly struggling for

the right words, "that just kind of happened, you know? Dick and Jillian were both zombies. Becca made an effort to do everything she could for them, but she didn't intrude like you're implying. She'd drop by with food and discreetly clean the house while they ate. After a month, she coerced Jillian into driving into town a couple of times a week to shop and have lunch. Every now and then she called me to suggest I invite Dick to play golf. She wasn't stalking him; she was just being thoughtful."

And I was a strong contender for the Republican nomination for the presidency. "But four months, Sid? That's hardly enough time to work through grief, especially if he was as overwhelmed as you've said he was. Then again, he bounced right back after Becca's death, didn't he? Three months later he was picking up women at the bank. He's either as resilient as a new tennis ball or is putting on his own little act."

Sid stood up. "I think you'd better leave." Rather than angered, he seemed shaken and deeply disturbed. He went to the window to stare at the lake, his hands clenched behind his back, his neck muscles tensed, his jaw quivering.

I let myself out and drove back toward Dick's house and Dunling Lodge, trying to filter out the facts from Sid's romanticized version of the story. Very little of what I'd heard from him—or from anyone else—was based on facts. Everyone seemed determined to live in a gilded fairy tale in

which all motives were pure, all actions uncalcu-
lated. Becca, I thought with a sigh, must have felt
as though she were conning a kindergarten class.
First Marilyn at the airport, visibly in need of a
firm hand and a sympathetic ear. Scottie, as easily flattered as a beauty contestant. Jan, timidly
hovering at the edge of the social circle. Agatha
Anne and Georgiana, eager to add recruits to
the cause—especially when the recruit met their
fashion criterion. Jillian, dumpy and plain, dazzled by that same criterion. Dick, immobilized
with grief. Anders, an enthusiastic womanizer
who lived in a conveniently remote area.

I stopped in the middle of the road as I replayed
Anders's remarks about the day of the accident.
I'd asked ever so casually if Becca had been at his
trailer. He'd replied that he couldn't remember,
but had added with preciseness that Agatha Anne
and Georgiana had been there and stayed until
dark, discussing the release date of a red-tailed
hawk. He had a curiously selective memory. Surely
Gannet had questioned everyone remotely con-
nected with the deceased woman, tracking her
movements prior to the accident, demanding details. He would have done so the next morning, if
not that same evening, and he would not have accepted such a casual answer.

Anders had lied to me, and behind his dismis-
sive "of that I am not sure" was deliberation. The
only incentive for lying was to hide something,
and the obvious something was an affair. Becca

had a superficially virtuous reason for her trips to the trailer. With the windows open, she and Anders could hear a car or truck grinding down the hill several minutes before its arrival. Anyone approaching from the rear would set off an avian alarm system more effective than a siren.

I came to an unpleasant realization. If Dick suspected as much, he had yet another motive for murder. Anders lacked one. I'd caught him in a clench with Agatha Anne, who might have been jealous. Blowing up Becca and the boat seemed a bit extreme, however, and apt to discourage the resumption of an amorous relationship. And she'd dutifully reported the propane leak hours before the accident. As a would-be assassin, she had a lot to learn.

This not-all-that-improbable affair could explain a lot of minor mysteries. Said topic could have caused the fight at the cocktail party, if either Becca or Anders had done something indiscreet that confirmed Dick's suspicions. I'd seen no symptoms that he was a violently possessive man, but I didn't know him well and nothing to provoke such an emotion had taken place during my visits. Luanne sure as hell wasn't going to pass along any insights. If Dick had snapped, he could have done exactly what Gannet had suggested: tamper with the propane line, fake the report, and later silence Bubo, who was a logical contender for the unidentified witness.

The tea in my stomach seemed to curdle as I

considered how neatly it all fit together. The only puzzle that remained was the identity of the vile sneak who'd pushed me into the lake. Luanne had said that Dick called her at eleven-thirty. She may have been blinded by passion, but I doubted she was unable to tell time—or tell the truth. Turnstone Lake was a vast puddle of many thousand acres, and Dick would have needed time to take his boat to its far end and find a telephone.

A car sped around the corner, braked abruptly, lurched toward the ditch, and skidded to a stop inches from my bumper. Gannet's face was visible for a moment before dust drifted down, coating both our windshields like a lacy brown blanket. A car door slammed, footsteps crunched the rocks, and my door was yanked open.

"I thought I told you to stay at Cissel's house," Gannet said with what I felt was inordinate exasperation.

"I was on my way back there, Captain Gannet. I needed to make a long-distance call, so I went to use the phone at the convenience store. You really shouldn't drive so recklessly on these narrow roads. It's bad for your blood pressure."

He ignored my solicitude. "I need you to follow me to the sheriff's office. I've arrested Cissel for murder, and now it's time for formal statements from all the witnesses. You, Mrs. Malloy, are at the top of the list. I hope you take that as a compliment."

"Why did you arrest him?"

"Because he's guilty. We went down to Horseshoe Bend Marina, where he left his boat last night. The engine had recovered miraculously and started right up. Unless the elves worked on it in the dark hours of the morning, there was never anything wrong with it. Cissel claimed to be baffled. He claims to be baffled about a lot of other things, too, like why his car was seen at Blackburn Creek and why there was a phone call made from his house in town to the lake house."

"Was he home at the pertinent time?"

Gannet glowered down at me, huffing and puffing as though he'd like to blow my car into a tree. "I'm not in the mood to stand in the middle of the road and answer your questions. You can follow me voluntarily, or I can charge you as a material witness and give you a lift in the backseat of my car. You may not like it. A couple of days ago I took in an old geezer who vomited all over the floor. I haven't had time to clean it up."

I wasn't finished. "Dick Cissel is not a stupid person. He must have known you'd examine the boat. Why would he lie about something so easy to disprove?"

Captain Gannet declined to answer my astute question and repeated the two options. He sounded belligerent enough to stuff me into his trunk as if I were a sack of laundry, so I agreed to follow him in my own car. He failed to express gratitude for my cooperation, but he was not in an appreciably courteous mood. Nor did he take my advice about his driving.

The sheriff's office was located in a small town twenty or so miles away. Gannet had disappeared inside before I'd found a place to park among the official vehicles and the pickup trucks, all of which sported militant NRA bumper stickers. Landscaping consisted of eroded asphalt, beer cans, and weeds alongside the building. I had a foreboding feeling that it was not my kind of place.

Within an hour, I found myself in a cell less charming than any vomit-splattered backseat. The stench was abrasive enough to make my eyes sting. I decided not to attempt to identify the individual elements involved, and instead assessed the decor. One metal bunk with a thin, stained mattress. A porcelain sink with cracks like a spiderweb. A genuine spiderweb beneath it. Dried bugs along the perimeter of the concrete floor. Everything was gray or brown, with nary a fuchsia throw pillow in sight. They definitely needed the name of Agatha Anne's interior designer, I concluded as I sat on the edge of the bunk.

The incarceration was the result of statements taken earlier from two gentlemen purportedly named Noddy and Martin. Their last names had been mentioned, but I was hardly in the mood to hunt them up in the telephone directory to thank them for their contribution. Noddy and Martin, it seemed, had been fishing near the dock at the Blackburn Creek Marina the previous evening. Around eleven, they'd determined they were out of beer and sandwiches. The engine was balky, they admitted, and they'd made a great deal of noise before they coaxed it into life. Noddy and Martin were quite sure they'd awakened everyone within a mile of the dock. One of them had added that he felt like he was setting off Chink-made firecrackers. It sounded like a remark someone named Noddy would make.

Gannet was not amused by this minor omission in my earlier recitation or in the formal statement I'd given in an inhospitable interrogation room. Unwilling to even listen to my explanation (which surely I could have concocted after some thought), he'd personally escorted me down a grungy corridor and held open the cell door. He'd slammed and locked it, too.

No one came down the corridor for what felt like a very long time. Dick was somewhere in the building, but I'd not spotted him and there'd been no noise from the cells on either side of mine. I propped my head on my fists and contemplated my hostile reception by Turnstone Lake, home of the sleekly rich. From the moment I'd turned off the highway and entered the maze of roads and trails, I'd been in one sort of trouble or another. I'd been insulted and assaulted. I'd been smirked at and spied on. I'd subsisted on cold lasagna.

I vowed to take down the bird feeder outside

my living-room window—and to eat chicken
and turkey on a more regular basis, along with
pheasant, quail, and Cornish hen when the opportunity arose. If eagleburgers ever came in vogue,
I'd stand at the front of the line and hold out my
plate.

In the meantime, there was nothing to do. The
graffiti on the wall were symptomatic of the sorry
state of rural education—even the crudest basic
four-letter words were misspelled. Gannet had
laughed nastily at my demand to be allowed a
phone call; my only hope for bail resided with
Luanne, who might notice my car if she came to
the office to rescue Dick. My mind was too be-
numbed to ponder the situation. I lay down along
the edge of the filthy mattress and mutely be-
seeched whatever vermin resided in the cell to do
only minimal damage. Eventually, I drifted into a
restless sleep.

Amid much clanking and squeaking, the door
opened. I awoke instantly, but I kept my eyes
closed and waited to find out if I was to be interrogated by Gannet or offered bread and water.

"Claire?"

I squeezed my eyes closed and tried to keep my
breathing slow and steady. The last time I'd been
in jail, I'd expected a certain person to rush to my
salvation. He'd sent an underling. Now, when I
truly had no desire to see or speak to him, he'd
abandoned his guests and galloped across the
county. Drat.

"What happened to your football game?" I muttered, declining to play the gracious hostess.

"It's still going on, I guess. Would you stop growling and sit up, please? I feel as though I've intruded on a hibernating bear."

I refused to move. "That's exactly what I'm doing—hibernating. I'm sure the guys need you more than I, so why don't you go home and worry about this first and ten business?" I put enough emphasis on "the guys" to let him know I'd overheard some of the background chatter.

Peter's rumble of irritation was familiar, as was his frigid tone. "If you insist, I'll go back to Farberville and start the charcoal. Captain Gannet may well go to his house and do the same thing. One thing he won't do is release you until tomorrow morning at the earliest. Your stubbornness is going to lead to eighteen more hours in here, Claire. By the way, you may be getting a roommate before too long. They have to get her sedated and hosed off before they lock her up."

"You're awfully crabby today," I said as I sat up and smoothed my hair. "Where's that renowned Rosen sense of humor?"

"This is not the time for jokes. You're in bad trouble with these boys, and I have no jurisdiction whatsoever. They barely grasp the concept of professional courtesies."

I looked at him and shook my head. "Perhaps if you weren't wearing tattered gym shorts and a grass-stained shirt, they'd take you more seriously.

Those sneakers must have come from a Dumpster. What happened to your shining armor?"

Peter's usually mild eyes were flickering. There were lots of white teeth in sight, but there was nothing sincere about his smile. "Listen, I left my guests and drove here as fast as I dared to try to help you, but you're behaving as if I were your sworn enemy. I didn't tell Gannet to lock you up—although if I were in his place, I might have done the same thing. Cops are testy when they're told lies during a murder investigation."

"I didn't tell a single lie," I said coolly. "I forgot one tiny detail, that's all. Gannet needs to be sedated and hosed off." I stood up and forced a measure of warmth, if not enthusiasm, into my voice. "I really do appreciate your coming, Peter. Can we go now?"

"All I know is that Gannet's willing to talk to you one last time before he flings the cell key into the lake. Don't keep pushing him. The mention of your name turns him rabid." He put his hands on my shoulders and shook me gently. "I realize you've never listened when I've tried to convince you to stay out of official investigations, and I've done it so many times we both know the exact phrasing. I have no influence with Gannet, nor does my superior or anyone else on the Farberville police force. Constitutional rights can get lost out here in the woods. The legal system is a combination of rewards and family favors, and outsiders don't have a chance."

"I didn't opt to spend the weekend making Gannet's life miserable. I came to help Luanne. As distasteful as the idea may be, I'm beginning to agree with Gannet that Dick Cissel was implicated in his second wife's death. I cannot allow Luanne to find herself in the same predicament, or in this case, the same funeral parlor." I stopped, aware that my face was flushed and my eyes blinking too rapidly. I tried to laugh, but my mouth was dry and the sound that emerged sounded like a pitiful little cough. "Can we go, warden?"

I'm not sure if what crossed his face was frustration or tenderness, but the ensuing behavior seemed to suggest the latter. For that matter, I wasn't sure if my motive was gratitude or a sudden realization that I did care for him, even at his crabbiest. The cell stayed steamy until we put a few inches between us and grinned like a couple of bashful, embarrassed adolescents. Had the mattress not been so unappealing . . .

Gannet sat at his desk, which was covered with photographs and diagrams. He stolidly acknowledged my meek apology for the oversight. I insisted that I had not heard a second boat, but I had a feeling he thought I was lying to protect Dick. After a bit of wrangling, he informed me that I could return to Farberville, as long as I remained at his beck and call. I had an urge to ask him if he actually had a beck, and if so, could I see it, but the specter of the cell overruled it. Peter made the obligatory noises of gratitude and hustled me out the door.

"Did you see those diagrams?" I asked Peter as he opened my car door. "They relate to the boat explosion, not Bubo's murder. Someone has measured the distance from the hillside behind the marina office to a point out in the lake. Is there some kind of radio device that could have caused the propane to explode?"

"No."

"Oh, come on," I said, pleased with my nascent theory. "What if you could fiddle with a cigarette lighter so that it would ignite when you punched a button?"

"No."

"There's probably some sort of stove in the cabin. Couldn't you do something so that the burner would come on and set off the propane?"

"No."

Clearly he was not in the mood to work on this newest brainstorm. None of the Turnstone Lake residents had seemed knowledgeable in electronics, but I would ask around and then explore the possibilities. If it came down to it, I could call an electronics store and quiz an employee.

"Never mind," I said as I looked up sweetly. "I'm going by Dick's house to grab my suitcase and pick up the girls. Do you have time to come along before you go back to town? Luanne's likely to be gnawing her toenails by now. She needs some support."

"No."

"Have a nice day," I said, then rolled up the window and drove away.

10

Dick's lake house was unlocked, but also uninhabited. I scribbled a note to Luanne, packed my things, and left before Jillian materialized in the shadows. The girls were sitting on their luggage in front of Dunling Lodge; they flung all of it and themselves into the car before I'd come to a full stop. I waited outside the convenience store long enough for them to snatch up an array of junk food and a six-pack of sodas, and was regaled with chomping and slurping for the remainder of the drive. Their grumbles were made through mouthfuls of chips, and were therefore mostly unintelligible. My car resembled a portable garbage bin by the time I'd dropped off Inez and pulled into the garage below the duplex.

"Are you going back next weekend to start earning money?" I asked Caron as we carried our bags upstairs.

Her lower and now well-nourished lip shot out. "Yeah, we said we would. It wouldn't be so horrible if we got to drive the barge, but we don't get to because we might"—she mimicked Agatha Anne's honeyed voice and plastic smile— "inadvertently go too close to the aerie and frighten Mama and Papa Eagle and all the little eaglets." She resumed her more typical mien of martyrdom, replete with rolling eyes, sighs, and an occasional gulp of despair. "We have to lead groups on bird walks. I was assigned the three-mile-long Mallard Trail, so I get to point at ducks while we go slogging through the swamp. 'Oooh,' I'll squeal, 'a duck!' Everybody will crumple with excitement, and I'll have to do CPR on a five-hundred-pound bald guy while I drag him to the lodge. Agatha Anne literally was gloating when she assigned it to me, then gave Inez the Mockingbird Trail, which is only a mile long and doesn't go anywhere near the swamp. I'm going to have nightmares about things that go quack in the night!"

"Hmmm," I said.

"And there's a sign by the door that says tipping is against the rules. It's in all the pamphlets, too. What kind of Atheist Organization Is This? I'd believe Agatha Anne was a communist if I hadn't seen her diamond-and-ruby Republican Party pin."

"It's a nonprofit organization," I said, wondering why I bothered to use a phrase Caron found ludicrous, if not obscene. She harrumphed and snorted until I'd unlocked the front door, then dropped her luggage in the living room and fled to her bedroom to share her resentment with whomever she could entice to the opposite end of the telephone line.

I took a long bath to wash away any lingering redolence from my interminable confinement, dined on nuked food, and was settled on the sofa with a glass of scotch and the Sunday newspaper when the telephone rang. I ignored it.

Caron came to the doorway. "It's for you," she said accusingly. "Try to keep it as brief as possible, okay? Traci's going to call me back as soon as her father gets finished talking to some man in someplace ridiculous like Frankfurt. I was in the middle of telling her about all the frat boys we met out on the lake when the line blipped. Unlike some of us, Traci has call waiting."

"How many frat boys did you meet?"

She narrowed her eyes. "Some."

"Oh, really?" When no further enlightenment was proffered, I picked up the receiver. "Hello?"

"What happened to you this afternoon?" Luanne began indignantly. "I waited and waited, then finally drove over to the marina to see if you'd gone for another swim. A pubescent deputy said he hadn't seen you, but that Captain Gannet was looking for you. When I got back to the house, who should drive up but the jolly old captain himself, his chubby cheeks as rosy as Santa's. He took great pleasure in telling me Dick was in custody, charged with two counts of first-degree murder. To my astonishment, Jillian fell apart, and it took an hour of tea and sympathy before she calmed down."

"Jillian fell apart?" I said. "She's the least emotional woman I've ever met. It's hard to imagine her shedding a tear if a truck ran over her foot."

"Trust me—she did. She was edgy when she arrived back here in the afternoon, but when Gannet told her he'd arrested her father, I thought she was going to expire on the spot. Neither Gannet nor I could make much sense of her blubbering and moaning, although she did manage to convey that she was positive Dick hadn't killed Becca. She went through an entire box of tissues before she staggered off to her bedroom. I kept thinking you'd show up, but nooo . . ."

"I left a note on the breakfast bar."

"Why would I look for a note on the breakfast bar?" she snapped. After a pause, she said in a more conciliatory tone, "All right, I found it. So you left a note."

"Are you going to stay at the lake?"

"No, there's no reason for me to do that. I called the sheriff's office, but Gannet wouldn't speak to me. He did send the message that Dick would remain in custody until the end of the week and I wouldn't be allowed to communicate with him. Jillian called a lawyer, who's going there as soon as he can tomorrow. I'm afraid that if I stay, I'll be beset by Agatha Anne and Sid, Georgiana,

Livia Dunling, and whoever else wants to hear the gruesome details. Besides, I need to water my houseplants."

"I don't think Gannet can hold Dick that long without a bail hearing, but that's what lawyers are for." I took a deep breath and an equally deep swallow of scotch, then told her how I'd spent the afternoon.

Rather than expressing horror at my ordeal, Luanne sighed and said, "Now that you've been in that awful place, you should be all the more eager to help me get Dick out of Gannet's evil clutches. By the way, I need to ask a small favor. At some point tomorrow I want to run by Dick's house in town and pick up some books and the mail. I can take them with me when I go back in a day or two, and surely Gannet will let Dick have them after they've been X-rayed for machine guns and hacksaws. Then I started thinking about it. It sounds so innocuous, but the idea of going inside this dark, empty mansion all by myself—"

"Tonight you'll go inside a dark, empty apartment, and tomorrow morning you'll go inside a dark, empty store. In both situations you will flick on the lights to banish the ghosties and ghoulies. You're way too old to worry about things that go quack in the night."

I hung up. The telephone rang almost instantly, but Caron picked it up in her bedroom

and began to chirp and chortle. I turned to the
obituary section to see how the competition (in
the human race) was faring.

Business was deadly the next morning. I drank
coffee, dusted, rearranged racks to confuse my
customers, and finally went into the office to ar-
gue via long distance with a particularly snippety
shipping clerk who insisted that her invoices were
accurate. She seemed to feel the problem lay in
my lack of visual acuity rather than in her indeci-
pherable numbers. Our conversation ended on
what might be described as a crescendo of acri-
mony.

Invigorated, I refilled my coffee mug, then
found the telephone directory under a stack of
unopened letters with cellophane windows, and
cheerfully resumed meddling in an official investigation. Half an hour later I closed the directory.
No one at any of the local electronics stores was
willing to explain how to design a device to blow
up a boat. On the other hand, no one flatly denied it was possible. Gannet was convinced Dick
was in town half an hour before the explosion,
making the bogus call to Becca. The lake was an
hour's drive, at best. Someone else had clutched
the clicker.

I returned to the front room and climbed onto
the stool behind the counter, took the deck of
cards out of the drawer, aimed it at the door, and
pressed my thumb down. "Boom!" I said, idly sup-
plying the sound effects while wishing I could be

sure the technology existed. I wondered if I could pose as a writer doing research and find someone at the college willing to share the methodology of my hypothetical death ray in exchange for a mention in the acknowledgments. "Boom," I said again, this time symbolically obliterating a cockroach beneath the classics.

"Boom, boom," whispered a voice from within the paperback section. It was not an echo.

This was not the infamous dark, empty mansion. The sky was blue and pedestrians paraded down the sunny side of the street. Traffic was light, but there were enough cars and trucks to pervade the environs with noxious fumes. I took the feather duster and cautiously eased around the end of the rack; if worse came to worst, I was prepared to tickle the intruder into submission.

Sitting cross-legged on the floor was my semi-regular science fiction freak, a woolly old hippie with unnaturally bright eyes behind wire-rimmed glasses and enough breadcrumbs in his wispy beard to provide dinner for a flock of starlings. He wiggled his fingers at me, then turned the page of whatever he was reading and bent over it as if he were licking the words off the page.

Lowering my lethal weapon, I asked, "How long have you been here?"

"Not too long. You were in the back room, yelling at somebody named Jennifer. I didn't want to interrupt on account of I met Jennifer at the last World Con and she was the scariest Speculumian warrior-queen I'd ever seen. She was like six feet tall, and dressed in a studded black leather bikini and a hood. Speculumians are short and squatty, but when I told her so, she jerked me up over her head and threw me at a Gorget dude. He threw me back at her, and I ended up being intergalactic ballast for ten minutes. It was not my best convention."

"I don't think it's the same Jennifer," I said, then paused to consider the call. "But I may be mistaken. In any case, I was on the telephone. Did the bell above the door jangle when you came in?"

"You were yelling really loud," he said apologetically. He replaced the book, stood up, and ambled out the door. This time the jangle was audible.

Caron arrived at noon. Her hair was uncombed and her face devoid of makeup. She wore torn shorts, a T-shirt from years past, and rubber flip-flops. Clearly she was dressed for a particular role, but I couldn't predict what it would prove to be. Anything was possible.

"I called the high school to make sure I'm signed up for second-semester driver's ed," she announced in the sepulchral tone of an elderly tragedienne in a faded crinoline gown, standing in the doorway of a dusty ballroom. "Coach Scoter's not going to teach it because his wife had surgery or something. They're trying to find someone else. With my luck, it'll be some bufflehead who believes in separation of the sexes.

Louis and I won't be allowed in the car at the same time, much less the backseat."

"Bufflehead?" I repeated carefully and very blankly. "Is this some sort of reference to a bison?"

"A bufflehead is a duck, Mother. It's found in salt bays and estuaries. The male, known for its squeaky whistle, has a greenish-purple head. The book did not explain why this color combination is referred to as 'buffle,' but I was not intrigued enough to ask Agatha Anne."

"It does have a nice ring to it, dear. Do you happen to know anyone who builds model airplanes or cars that are operated by some sort of remote control device?"

"Why would I know anyone that totally nerdy?" Having deftly dealt with my question, Caron slumped to the floor and leaned against the self-help rack. Her breathing grew raspy, but it would have to halt altogether before I would feel any alarm. "Inez called to say that she talked to Louis's sister last night, and she said that Louis is going to a swimming party at Rhonda's house on Saturday night. Everyone's going to be there, except the total nerds and maybe Allison Wade, who made some catty remark about Rhonda's Monumental Buttocks. If you ask me, they ought to be a national park." She slithered further down so she could gaze up piteously at me, and the wheezing became more pronounced as she resumed her earlier role. "The total nerds,

Allison—and Inez and me. We'll be stuck at the lake all weekend, eating bran and listening to twaddle about eaglets. Unless, of course, someone could drive us here after the last tour of the day and take us back to the lake after the party."

"I'll ask around for volunteers, but I wouldn't count on it if I were you." I opened the directory to the yellow pages and hunted for the heading "Nerds, electronic."

"Or we could hitchhike," said a despondent voice.

"And find yourselves grounded in perpetuity. You've already blackmailed me once this week. Part of our bargain was that you would accept your responsibilities as an employee of the Dunling Foundation and carry through on them."

Caron opted to change the subject rather than explore the components of our agreement. "The first tour starts at seven on Saturday morning and the same on Sunday. While everybody else is sleeping until noon because they went to a fabulous party, I'll be slogging through the swamp."

"And earning ten dollars an hour," I reminded her before I was treated to a replay of the scenario. "You're always referring to Rhonda's little brother as nerdy. Does he know anything about electronics?"

"He collects gum wrappers and swizzle sticks." She slunk away to collapse on the sidewalk and die before the horrified pedestrians, or to call a child-abuse agency and turn me in. I resorted to the hum and drum of bookselling for the remainder of the afternoon. I was checking to make sure the back door was locked when Luanne burst into the office.

"Claire! You must come with me!"

"Don't be a bufflehead," I countered. "The only thing I must do is close the store and go home. I may decide to pick up Chinese food later, but that does not fall in the category of essential."

"I went by Dick's house. As soon as I opened the front door, I heard another door close somewhere in the house. Fools may rush in, but I sure as hell didn't. Please come back with me, Claire."

"Call the police," I said promptly. Despite my superior judgment and a lifelong habit of reading fiction, I'd been known to prowl inside what I'd supposed were empty houses. Invariably, the results had been unpleasant, and I'd sworn off such behavior (thus precluding a career in real estate and/or cat burglary).

"I can't call the police," Luanne said with more despair than Caron had ever manufactured for my entertainment. "Dick would never forgive me if I invited them to search his house, especially now."

"Because they might find additional proof of his guilt?"

"There is no proof of his guilt! You've had several encounters with Gannet. He'd do anything to hang Dick, including plant evidence or invent faceless witnesses who just happened to have been at the right place at the right time." She came forward as if to clutch my arm, forcing me to retreat into the tiny bathroom made tinier by the inclusion of boxes of books, piles of outdated catalogs, and cleaning equipment. "Dick values his privacy. He couldn't bear the idea of people pawing through his things. Please come with me. We'll just make sure all the doors and windows are locked, grab the books and the mail, and be out in three minutes."

"Unless we encounter a drug addict."

Luanne nibbled her lip and pretended to re-call the moment. "I'm pretty sure it was the back door. Whoever was inside heard me drive up in front, panicked, and left. He's probably halfway down here by now."

I ignored the sharp edge of the sink and shook my head resolutely. If I'd had the feather duster, I would have shaken it, too. "I am not going into a house that might have an inmate in a closet. If you heard someone, you should call the police."

"Maybe I just thought I heard a door close. It was just a tiny sound that could have come from a squirrel on the roof—or even more likely, a bird flying into a window. They do that all the time at the lake. Jillian told me that Becca used to put them in a basket and carry them to tall weeds so they could recover without being attacked. I tried once, but the bird glared at me as if it fully in-tended to peck me in the eye. I left it for the cats."

"If you heard a bird, then you don't need me to

hold your hand," I said, making the logical leap despite the fact I was cornered by a lovesick—and consequently demented—woman. "You can't have it both ways, Luanne. I'm not going to Dick's house to nurse a cross-eyed bird, and I'm not going there to startle a drug addict with an automatic weapon and a bad attitude. Call the police, or call the Humane Society."

"Okay, I didn't want to have to say this, because I may be wrong and I don't want to get an innocent party in trouble. When I was backing over the azaleas in my haste to leave, I thought I saw Anders Hammerqvist drive by. He could have been coming from a side street alongside the house. Can you think of a reason why he would have been in the house?"

"No," I said, but suddenly it seemed intriguing to see if we could discover one. "I'll take my car and follow you."

Dick Cissel's lake house was large and gracious, but his town house was indeed a mansion. Luanne had implied it was a towering Gothic structure, but it was a pseudo-Tudor tucked among pseudo-Early Americans, pseudo-Victorians, and a disturbing number of pseudo-Italian villas. The foreign cars and limousines were genuine, as were the riding lawn mowers driven by olive-skinned yardmen. Their trucks and vans were the only blemishes in this otherwise impeccable setting. Those and the flattened azaleas beside the driveway, that is.

Luanne had the key in her hand as I joined her on the stoop. "I borrowed Dick's," she said as she unlocked the door and stepped back to allow me to walk into the loving embrace of a cocaine-crazed psychopath.

The marble-floored foyer was larger than my entire apartment. Mail was piled in a basket on a mahogany table beneath a mirror. I left Luanne sorting through it and ventured into a living room of overwhelming formality. I dismissed the very concept of guests sitting on the straight-backed chairs or the delicate sofas and love seats.

I continued into the next room and gaped at the dining-room table, which could accommodate two dozen diners. The centerpiece of silk flowers was nearly high enough to brush a chandelier that would wipe out all the diners if it fell at a judicious moment. There were many mirrors; guests of both sexes could pause every few feet to compliment themselves on the success of their packaging.

In the kitchen, also larger than my apartment, I found a coffee cup in the sink and several plates in the dishwasher. This was to be expected, since Dick stayed in town during the week. Having committed myself to a full-blooded prowl, I opened the refrigerator. Among the trendier products I saw a pizza box, confirming that the wealthy also had their moments when junk food appealed more than caviar. The pizza itself, mundane pepperoni rather than artichoke hearts and smoked salmon, appeared fairly fresh. Jillian must have ordered it Saturday evening, I thought as I roamed through the remaining downstairs rooms and returned to the foyer.

"No killers on this floor," I said brightly. "The back door and all the French doors are locked."

Luanne looked up with watery eyes. "These are magazines for Becca. I guess Dick didn't think to cancel the subscriptions—or couldn't bring himself to do it."

"Is there any personal mail addressed to her?"

"No, just *Town & Country* and *Vanity Fair.* Shall we check the upstairs before we go?"

We began at the top of the stairs. Jillian's bedroom was as prim as a convent cell (although much vaster), and the adjoining bathroom was sterile. The master suite, now occupied by only the master, had begun a gradual transition to a more masculine ambience. The walls were still peach and the drapes lined with sheers, but socks hung out of half-opened drawers, soiled shirts were piled in a corner, and the bed, a king-sized affair with built-in reading lights and dainty bedside tables, was sloppily made, as if done as an afterthought.

"This was Becca's dressing room," Luanne said without enthusiasm as she opened a door. Inside was a lavishly equipped bathroom, complete with bidet and color-coordinated hair dryer and telephone. In an alcove, a marble Jacuzzi glinted in sunshine that streamed through the skylight above it. The numerous plants looked as though they'd at one time thrived, but now some of them needed attention and a few hearty words of encouragement.

The closet was immense and as tightly organized as a NASA control room, Rods sagged from the weight of innumerable dresses, skirts, jackets, and blouses, and at one end were three full-length fur coats. Special racks had been constructed to hold every imaginable style and color of shoe, from bright sandals to dainty satin slippers. On shelves were round hatboxes, purses, plastic covers for folded sweaters, and neatly furled umbrellas should the weather dare threaten a silken shoulder or linen cuff. The very concept of one person possessing all of this was staggering; I'd been in department stores with a less extensive inventory.

Luanne nudged me out of my stupor, and as we returned to the hallway, said, "Jillian promised Dick that she'd pack up everything and send it to the Salvation Army thrift shop, but she keeps putting it off."

"I can't imagine why," I said as I followed Luanne into an office with a large desk, bookshelves, and a filing cabinet. It was all very gentlemanly, with heavy brass embellishments, cumbersome leather chairs, and paintings of ships in storm-tossed seas.

I realized Luanne was staring at something hidden by the open door and moved beside her. Centered on the wall was a large oil painting of a blond woman dressed in a shimmery blue gown. Her hair was swept back with diamond barrettes, and around her neck was a diamond-and-sapphire necklace. Her full lips curled enigmatically, and her eyes were dreamy. Her cheeks glowed with a maidenly blush. Her long, slender fingers held a single flower.

"Am I allowed three guesses?" I asked.

"She really was beautiful, wasn't she?" Luanne murmured as she sat down behind the desk and straightened a few papers. "Not only beautiful, but kind and generous and compassionate. No wonder Dick was so besotted."

I studied the portrait for a clue to Becca's true character, but found myself mesmerized by her fragile beauty and precariously close to returning her smile. I turned my back on her. "Why is the portrait in here? I'd have expected to find it in the living room above the fireplace."

"Dick wanted to hang it there, but Becca insisted that it be in here. She initially refused to pose or even meet the artist, and he had to threaten to have it done from a photograph if she wouldn't cooperate. Hanging it here was a compromise. According to him, she was actually very shy and insecure, which is why she preferred to listen to other people rather than talk about herself."

"Give me a break," I said ungraciously, then went back downstairs and into the living room to envision the portrait above the fireplace. Perhaps Becca had declined to allow it to be hung there because it would clash with the decor, I decided without much interest as I inspected all the windows to see that they were locked. I did the same with the ones in the dining room, then reentered the kitchen and continued my mission.

As I passed by the sink, I glanced at the coffee cup. From this perspective I could see a tiny line of color on the rim. There was only a trace of what appeared to be lipstick, but I was afraid to touch it and inadvertently wipe it away. I replaced the cup and turned my attention to the coffeemaker. The glass pot had been rinsed and left inverted to dry on the counter, but the circular plate on the coffeemaker was warm.

Jillian had returned to the lake the previous afternoon. The coffeemaker should have long since cooled completely. I reexamined the pot and found a few beads of water along the aluminum band.

"Claire, I'm ready to go," Luanne called from the foyer.

So was I, frankly. "Someone has been in the house," I told her as I joined her. I explained about the warm coffee maker and other incriminating evidence. "Unless Jillian came back here this morning, it looks as though another woman has been here. Could it have been a housekeeper?"

"I called Jillian earlier and she said she spent the morning at the foundation office. The housekeeper might have taken advantage of an empty house to indulge in a coffee break, but she would have tidied up the bedrooms and put her cup in the dishwasher." She ran her finger across the surface of the mahogany table. "And dusted. Anyway, she's away for the summer to visit relatives."

"There were no signs that someone broke into the house. Does anyone else have a key?"

"I don't think so," Luanne said as she sat on the bottom step and let the mail fall to the marble floor. "While I was sitting at Dick's desk, I thought I smelled cigarette smoke. Neither he nor Jillian smokes, so I assumed I'd imagined it."

The only person I'd seen smoking at Turnstone Lake was Captain Gannet; if he'd wanted inside the house, he would have gotten a search warrant. One of the women could be a secret smoker, but I could think of no reason why she might feel compelled to hide her habit by somehow sneaking into Dick's house.

Another thought occurred. "I'm surprised there's no security system in the house. If I were a burglar, I'd case this neighborhood at least once a week."

Luanne gave me a startled look. "I forgot all about it. The box is just inside the coat closet. There are motion detectors in every room, and if the code's not punched in within thirty seconds, the security company dispatches armed officers."

"I don't hear any sirens."

"They don't have sirens, but they come roaring up in less than five minutes. Last week Dick and I came home from a dinner that included two bottles of wine and a cognac. Dick kept punching in the wrong sequence, and we were giggling when two husky men pounded on the door. They did not giggle." She opened the closet door and pointed at a black box that resembled a calculator. "The red light isn't blinking. Someone turned it off."

"Maybe Jillian forgot to reset it when she left yesterday," I said.

"Maybe." Luanne closed the closet door and picked up the scattered letters. "This place is giving me the creeps. I'm beginning to feel as if your burglar is still in the house, crouched in the attic or hiding under a bed. Are you ready to go?"

We both made sure the front door was locked, then walked to our respective cars. "One more thing," I said. "Did you pretend to see Anders in order to lure me here?"

"The truck was red, the same shade as his. I caught a very brief glimpse of blond hair as it went past the end of the driveway. It looked like him, but I certainly wouldn't swear to it."

"Was he alone?"

"All I saw was the hair. He could have had the entire Supreme Court crammed in the passenger's side. I'm probably mistaken, anyway. There's no reasonable explanation for him to have come into the house."

My resolve crumbled like a stale cracker, and although I was likely to end up at the state prison, chopping cotton under the blazing sun and writing mournful letters to Peter Rosen from my rat-infested cell, I said, "Well, then, perhaps we'd better ask him."

11

I devoted the next morning to business as usual, which meant I had plenty of free time to concoct reasons why Anders had been in Dick's house. None of them were remotely plausible, I regret to say, especially ones that compelled him to wear lipstick while drinking coffee. Late in the morning Luanne called to report that a hearing to set bail was scheduled for the afternoon; Gannet's threat to keep Dick until the end of the week had been nothing more than backwoods bluster. Sid had volunteered to attend with his checkbook. She, of course, would be sitting in the middle of the front row in the courtroom.

"Did you ask Jillian about the security system?" I asked after she'd quit chattering about Dick.

"She still sounded extremely overwrought when she called me earlier, and I was afraid to say anything she might construe as an accusation. She takes pride in being efficient and methodical. Dick says Jan was like that, too, although without

Jillian's abrasiveness." She hesitated, then said, "It might be better if you ask her, Claire. I'm planning a little party to celebrate Dick's release. As soon as I get to the lake, I'll drive down to Anders's trailer and invite him. It'll give you a chance to kill two birds with one stone."

"Don't let anyone on the Dunling Foundation board hear you say that," I said as I contemplated the tedious drive to the lake. I'd lost too much business over the weekend to close the Book Depot one minute early, and it was vital to my accountant's mental as well as spiritual health that I open promptly the next morning and begin snatching customers off the sidewalk. But the case had evolved into the sort that made my nose twitch. Earlier I'd bemoaned the dearth of clues. Now I had so many I was awash in puzzle pieces, none of which fit together thus far.

"I'll see if I can persuade Caron to manage the store," I said. "If she agrees, I'll be there by six or so. I am coming home as soon as the birds have been stoned. If something happens to prevent it, I will carry a grudge far into the next century."

"As long as you don't refuse to be my matron of honor," Luanne said smugly.

"And disappoint the next Mrs. Bluebeard?"

The dial tone buzzed in my ear. I called the apartment, but Caron did not answer. An hour later, however, she trudged in, dressed in even sloppier clothes than the previous day. Her voice was hoarse as she said, "Allison Wade was invited to the party. I might as well pitch a tent at Turnstone Lake and dedicate my life to sorting pamphlets and pointing at ducks. As my brain degenerates, I'll begin to paddle around the creeks and quack at the moon."

I struggled not to smile and made a motherly noise of sympathy before saying, "I need to leave at five. If you'll cover for me, you can keep the profits from any books you sell until closing time."

"Gee, then I can buy a Jaguar just like Agatha Anne's. If I have any change, I'll get one for Inez, too."

"It might mean less time slogging through the swamp."

She wandered behind the paperback fiction rack to consider the offer. Every now and then I heard a desultory quack, but she finally emerged. "Will you guarantee ten dollars an hour?"

It was a losing proposition, but I nodded and retreated to the office before she realized she could have held out for more.

I arrived at the lake house shortly after six. The parking area was so jammed that I was obliged to park partway up the driveway, and I could hear laughter and music from the deck while I crunched my way to the house. "Hail, hail," I muttered as I went inside and found Luanne in the kitchen. She was not wearing an apron, but there was a smudge of flour on her chin and a potholder in her hand.

"Good, you made it," she said.

This seemed self-evident, so I ignored it. "May I assume Dick was released on bail?"

"The county prosecutor argued against it because of the gravity of the crimes. The lawyer kept harping on Dick's pristine past, his ties to the community, and his need to keep open the practice so that children can face the future with well-aligned little smiles. They finally settled on a hundred thousand. Sid cut a deal with a bail bondsman. The whole thing didn't last half an hour." She took an aluminum tray of bubbly little bundles from the oven and managed to set it on the stove without incident. "No, I didn't make these," she said in response to my cynical expression. "They were in a bag in the freezer. Jillian made them last week in case we had people by for drinks."

"Is she doing better?"

Luanne began to rummage through a cabinet stocked with silver and china platters. "I thought she'd be relieved once Dick was free, but she walked right past him, not saying a word, and drove away in her own car. That was at about four o'clock, and she hasn't been seen since then."

"That is odd," I said as I watched her transfer the canapés to a more suitable serving dish. "She was very protective of him the first time I was here. Why would she give him what amounts to a cold shoulder? Are you sure she doesn't think he's guilty?"

"When Gannet told her he'd arrested her father, she kept insisting between sobs and hiccups that he couldn't have killed Becca. I wanted to talk to her about it later, but she refused to unlock her door. Yesterday morning when I called to check on her, she hung up on me when I brought it up. She sat by herself at the hearing."

"Where was she at the time of Becca's accident?"

"I don't remember anybody mentioning where she was. I know Agatha Anne and Georgiana were at Anders's trailer earlier that afternoon. Dick was in town, as was Sid. I have no idea about anyone else."

"Do you think Jillian blew up the boat?" Dick asked as he came into the kitchen. He spoke pleasantly, but his eyes were definitely not smiling. "I don't recall that her college offered any undergraduate classes in explosives."

It did not seem the right moment to ask about ones in electronics. "No," I said. "I was just trying to get a clear picture of the day. I'm sure Jillian was doing whatever she ordinarily did."

"A clear picture of the day?" he said as he picked up a canapé, then let it drop like a tiny bomb. "Then you don't think it was an accident any more than Gannet does. Am I your leading suspect, too?"

"You're patently Gannet's," I said, sidestepping the question. "He has a substantive case against you. If I'm going to try to disprove it, I need to know the truth. You've been lying to Gannet—and to everyone else, including me."

Luanne was too aghast to speak. Dick took a half-empty bottle of wine from the refrigerator and two glasses from a cabinet, then gestured at me to follow him. I tried to smile reassuringly at her as we left the room, but she turned her back and began to attack the canapés with ill-disguised fury.

We went out the front door. He set the glasses on the hood of the Jaguar and wiggled out the cork. "I've been lying to Gannet," he said as he handed me a glass. "And to everyone else, including not only you but also perhaps myself. But I had nothing to do with the accident—or whatever it was—that killed Becca."

I regarded him over the rim of the wineglass. "Then let's talk about your story. You and Becca had an argument at a party at Dunling Lodge. What was it about?"

"Her spending. Some bills came to the office that day, but by the time I got here, we were already late for the party. It wasn't the best time to bring it up, but I had one drink too many and lost my temper."

"That doesn't play," I said, managing to sip wine and shake my head at the same time (my talents are boundless). "She applied for her Visa card in the hospital nursery, and she probably didn't miss a day of shopping the entire time you were married. What had she bought that made you so angry you had a public row? A yacht? A fur coat? A small country?"

"I don't remember. Some jewelry, maybe."

"Are you sure you weren't angry at her because you'd discovered she was having an affair with Anders?"

"We were happily married. I was in love with her and gave her whatever she wanted. Why would she have an affair with anyone?"

"I have no idea, Dick. I never went in for that kind of behavior when I was married, so I don't know what motivates so-called happily married spouses to risk everything for an illicit romp." I waited for a moment in case he had any suggestions, then continued. "Here's an idea. What if you pretended to be enraged by the bill so that you could make it known loudly that you were driving back to Farberville. That explains why you were parked on the hill above the marina after the party. Gannet thinks you were tampering with the propane tank, but I think you were watching the Dunling Foundation boat. How am I doing?"

He lifted his glass in a mock toast. "You're doing well."

"Of course I am. But why would Becca risk meeting someone at the marina?" I thought it over for a minute. "She couldn't invite Anders to your house because Jillian was there, and perhaps they felt it was risky for her car to be parked at the trailer that late. She probably thought the boat was safe, as long as they didn't disturb Bubo."

"You're good," he said with what I presumed was more sincere admiration. "Very good. Actually, I drove past Anders's trailer, but his truck was gone. Gannet's mystery witness saw my Rover on the hill, but failed to see Becca's convertible and Anders's truck parked farther down the road where it comes to a dead end. But I can't admit to him that I was there—unless I explain why. As long as I insist that Becca and I were veritable turtledoves, I have no motive to have killed her. Gannet comes from a neck of the woods where adultery used to be grounds for justifiable homicide; a few generations back, no doubt some branches were pruned off his family tree in that manner." He sat on the fender and rubbed his temples with his free hand. "I intended to divorce Becca, that's all. The next afternoon I called her to tell her so, but she wasn't there."

"Gannet said he'd found a call on your long-distance bill. If no one was home . . . ?"

"I left a message on the machine, telling her my intentions. When I arrived at the house, the light was still blinking. I was rewinding the tape when the deputy arrived at the front door."

"Did you tell this to Gannet?"

"A version of it, but he refused to believe I erased an innocuous message about the grocery list. I certainly didn't tell him that I'd just threatened to divorce my wife because she was having yet another affair."

I hadn't gotten that far in my theorizing. "Another affair?" I said.

Dick sagged to the point I was afraid he would slide off the fender onto the rocks. He hooked a heel on the bumper at the last second. "I'm going to tell you something that no one else knows—except the guilty party. You've heard Georgiana wailing about Barry's unidentified mistress? I'm almost positive it was Becca. I can't tell you when or why I began to wonder, but there was something different about her—and some ill-defined sense of intimacy between the two when they were in the same room. When I dropped heavy hints, she tearfully denied it and accused me of irrational jealousy, Barry took off for Key West the next week, so I let the matter rest." He shoved back his hair and gave me a pained look. "I wondered if I was paranoid, to be honest. Our sex life improved, if anything. She was still the gracious hostess and tireless worker. She made a conscientious effort to be friends with Jillian, who can be difficult at times. She was . . ."

"Perfect?"

"Yeah, perfect," he said bitterly.

"What do you know about her background? Did she grow up in Miami? Is her family there? What was her maiden name?"

"Henridge was her maiden name, or at least the one she was using when I first met her. She

grew up in one of the suburban towns in southern Florida, and her parents both died while she
was in high school. There were no grandparents
or siblings. She said she'd lost touch with her few
remaining relatives. She always spoke of them
with a hint of contempt in her voice. I don't think
she was too upset about it."

"What about her personal papers, like a passport or social security card?"

"Becca didn't even have a driver's license when
I married her. She was carrying everything in her
purse when she was mugged; she'd just emptied
her safe deposit box at the bank because she was
moving out of the state. I suggested she write for
a copy of her birth certificate in order to get a
passport, but she said she didn't want to go anyplace farther than here, where the only things she
had to watch out for were birds and butterflies.
She used to laugh about being mugged, but she
was still deeply upset."

"Listen, Dick," I said earnestly, "we need to
find out about Becca's past. Call a private investigation agency in Miami and have them dig up
as much as they can. They need to find out where
she went to school and where she worked afterward. Ask Marilyn Gordon for the precise date
she met Becca at the airport, then have the inves-
tigators check back issues of the newspapers for
details of the mugging. If there's a mention of
the hospital, they can confirm the dates she was
there."

"She's dead. What difference does any of that make? What matters now is for me to prove my innocence. Does it matter if Becca was a homecoming queen fifteen years ago or how badly she was beaten when she was mugged?"

"It might."

"Someone from her past killed her?"

Despite his skepticism, he deserved a straight answer. "I truly don't know, Dick." I slid off the fender and went inside. Out on the deck, Luanne was passing around the canapés to familiar faces. The Dunlings sat like royalty on the settee, while Georgiana and Agatha Anne were perched on the rail. Sid had cornered Anders and appeared to be demonstrating his golf swing. I eased into the party, exchanging greetings and waiting for the opportunity to have a private chat with Anders.

Livia beckoned to me. "Isn't it thrilling?"

"It certainly is," I said, glancing at her husband in hopes he would elaborate on the source of our mutual thrills. In response, he stood up and went to the bar.

"Oh, dear," murmured Livia, watching him. "He's so very preoccupied these days. I really must think of a way to rid the yard of that nasty groundhog. Not only do the gunshots alarm me, they positively terrify whatever hikers are within earshot. Just this morning, a group in a van turned around in the parking lot and roared away without so much as taking a single step down the Mallard Trail. We'll have an enormous crowd this weekend, naturally, and it will be chaos should Wharton break his promise and bring out his shotgun."

"Why are you expecting a crowd this weekend?" I asked, wondering how a certain facilitator would react should she be subjected to nonstop slogging.

"Because of the article to appear in the paper later this week, Claire. We were just talking about it, weren't we? I was opposed to it initially because the success of the breeding is our first concern, but Agatha Anne insisted that this is a unique opportunity for the public. She even sent fliers to church and civic groups in the adjoining counties, offering them a discount for advanced reservations. We're going to double ticket prices for the occasion, and take the barge to within a quarter mile of the aerie. Those with adequate binoculars will have a stirring sight awaiting them. We'll have lectures complete with slides and a tape recording of the squeaky cackle the adult eagles make when in a defense posture. You will be here for our Eagle Awareness weekend, won't you?"

"I haven't made any plans yet," I said. "It sounds as though the weekend will be profitable. Did Agatha Anne and Georgiana ever get the books straightened out on Saturday night? Caron mentioned that they'd spread everything out and were working hard."

"I don't think they did," she said unhappily. "I

volunteered Wharton's services, but they insisted that they would be finished by Friday. The Raptors Ball is so very vital to the continuation of the Dunling Foundation. If word gets out that we're in arrears with the caterer or the florist, people will be less inclined to be generous. There are many other equally worthy organizations, although none is so dear to my heart."

"Does Wharton have experience in accounting?"

"After thirty years in the military, he has experience in almost everything. His superiors were not always rational when making assignments. It's almost a policy to disregard training and expertise."

"What about electronics?" I said, crossing my fingers.

"What about it?" Wharton said from behind the settee.

"I was just thinking about those wonderful old war movies, where everyone barked into walkie-talkies to coordinate the attack," I said. It was inane, admittedly, but it was tough to invent anything better with a bald-headed vulture glaring down at me.

"I was in communications for a time," he said, "but we didn't have time to play with gadgets. We strung telephone wire, installed surveillance systems, that sort of thing. Any more questions, Mrs. Malloy?"

I excused myself and went inside to hide until

I felt less like an appetizing mound of flesh. After I'd washed my face in the bathroom, I opened the door of Jillian's bedroom. She had not returned. On the wall were photographs of her father, her mother, the two of them on a boat, and one of herself in a graduation gown. There were none of Becca.

I began a systematic search of the entire house. The only photographs I found were of Dick, Jillian, Jan, and some of the people currently nibbling canapés. I could not recall any shots of Becca at the house in town, for that matter—only the portrait in Dick's office. And that had been painted under protest.

Good-byes were being said on the deck. As I went out, Wharton was helping Livia down the steps to the yard. Sid was now demonstrating his swing to Dick, while Agatha Anne watched impatiently.

Luanne came to the door, carrying glasses and wadded paper napkins. "Did you have a chance to talk to Anders?" she asked me in a low voice.

"Not yet," I admitted. "Has he left?"

"Ten or fifteen minutes ago." She searched my face, her expression carefully neutral. "You and Dick were outside for quite a long time. Did you . . . discuss anything significant?"

"You'd better ask him," I said, unwilling to tell her that he'd further incriminated himself in my mind. "However, I'll go by Anders's trailer now and try to find out if he really was in Dick's house yesterday. I don't know how he could have gotten hold of a key, but it's possible he was using the house for an assignation. Do we have any idea where Agatha Anne was yesterday afternoon?"

Luanne shrugged. "I was in town. Do you suspect she and Anders are having an affair?"

I described the clinch I'd seen in the office, although I omitted my emotional reaction, which had been juvenile at best. "Try to find out if Agatha Anne went to Farberville to see the insurance agent or somebody like that. She gave an interview to the newspaper sometime during the last two days. You might ask Georgiana about it."

"Why do I get Georgiana while you're tackling Anders?" she asked.

"You're in love, remember?" I hurried across the living room before she could offer a caustic remark about my intermittent personal crises.

The only light inside the trailer seemed to be in the kitchenette, but my headlights flashed on the red truck parked in front. I carefully closed the car door so as not to disturb the patients in the backyard cages, and knocked timidly on the door of the trailer. Luanne had said he'd left only ten or fifteen minutes earlier, I thought as I waited. He hadn't wasted any time tumbling into bed.

I knocked more loudly. A light came on in the living room and the door opened a few inches. "Hi," I said. "I didn't get a chance to talk to you earlier. If it's not too much of a bother, I was hoping I could ask you a question or two."

"Sure," said Anders, although he did not open the door any wider. "The problem is that I am not wearing any clothes at this minute. If you will wait there, I will put some on and we will talk."

I lost the battle to rein in my imagination, and my face was noticeably warm when he returned and ushered me inside. He wore only the little bitty shorts, which only made things worse. I declined a glass of vodka and sat on the edge of a chair, my ankles crossed and my hands folded in my lap. Anders sprawled on the sofa and regarded me with amiable expectancy. There was just enough amusement on his face to convince me he could read my mind as if it were an open book (in the same genre as *The Joy of Sex*).

"I saw your truck in Farberville yesterday," I said bluntly. It wasn't technically true, but I needed to get to the point before I began to drool.

"You should have honked and waved at me. I would have invited you to lunch."

"It was late in the afternoon," I said, desperately trying to keep a squeak out of my voice. "You were pulling out of the street alongside Dick's house."

"I do not know where that is, so I cannot say that you are right or wrong. After I was finished with errands, I did drive around up in the hills where the rich people are living. The Gallinagos live in a very fine house. I have been there at a cocktail party preceding the Raptors Ball."

"Then you weren't inside Dick's house?"

He stiffened. "As I was telling you, I do not know where it is. I have no key. For that matter, I have no reason to be there. Dick was in jail, and I certainly would not be visiting Jillian. She is much too gloomy, like my *mormor*, my grandmother, who dressed in black for fifty years and went to sit in the church every morning."

I was almost certain he was lying. "We both know you were there, Anders. Who else was rolling around on the king-size bed with you? I know it's someone who wears lipstick and drinks coffee, and possibly likes pepperoni pizza after a"—I needed a word that would not cause me to turn any more crimson than I already was—"frolic."

He did his best to give me a look of immense bewilderment. "I am not understanding."

"How did Agatha Anne get a house key?" I asked aggressively. "And why did you two choose Dick's house? Was she afraid Sid might show up at hers unexpectedly?"

Anders's mouth fell open, and he gaped at me as if I'd confessed to owning a well-thumbed book of eagle recipes. "I am not sure what to say," he managed to whisper. "I do not wish to cause trouble for anyone, including Agatha Anne. Perhaps you are reading too much into our friendly embrace last weekend. There is something in my nature that leads me to show affection in such a way. She and I are only friends."

"In the same fashion you and Becca were friends? Dick told me that he suspected the two of you were having an affair. He staged the argument at the party so that you and Becca would think he'd gone back to town, but he didn't. He saw you at the marina."

We sat in silence. His forehead was creased, and beneath his golden tan, his face was ashen. He opened his mouth several times, but apparently was having no luck coming up with a credible explanation. "I think," he said at last, "that I will have some vodka. Are you sure you will not join me, Claire?"

"No, I'm driving back to town tonight."

He stood in the kitchenette and tossed down several glasses. I forced myself to watch his face rather than his hard, flat stomach and broad chest graced with downy blond hair. I barely noticed that in his haste to dress, he'd failed to button his little bitty shorts.

"Okay, then," he said as he replaced the bottle in the refrigerator and set the glass in the sink. "Becca and I did have an affair for about three months. Most times we were together here during the day, when she was supposed to be helping with the birds. On rare occasions, we were together on the boat that belongs to the Dunling Foundation. I felt it was too risky, but she seemed to enjoy it all the more because of the chance we might be caught."

"Did Bubo Limpkin know what was going on?"

"Not that I am aware." His shoulders rippled

elegantly as he shrugged. "He was the sort to make trouble, Bubo was."

I did a bit of calculation. If Becca's affair with Barry Strix had ended when he left town in December, she'd wasted no time finding a substitute. "When did you last see her?"

"We left the boat before dawn and went our separate ways. She was wishing to come to the trailer at noon." He stopped and licked a drop of vodka off the corner of his mouth. "I could not agree because I had a meeting with an officer from the state agency to arrange the transfer of an eagle to a facility in the southern corner of the state. I left here late in the morning and returned around four."

"And that's when Agatha Anne and Georgiana came?" I said. "Had they seen Becca at any time during the day?"

"I seem to think they mentioned that Becca had been at the foundation office part of the morning." He gave me a weak smile. "You should be asking them about this."

"Yes, indeed. Let's return to the topic of yesterday afternoon, shall we? Why in heaven's name did you and Agatha Anne meet at Dick's house?"

"They didn't," said Georgiana Strix as she came out of the bedroom, dressed only in one of Anders's shirts. "We did."

12

"Stay out of this," Anders said curtly and not at all melodiously. His accent could have been that of any ordinary Chicago gangster.

Georgiana shook her frizzy head. "Agatha Anne is my best friend. I can't let Claire spread rumors that might break up her marriage." She padded barefoot across the room and sat down next to him. Without makeup, her face was disturbingly bloodless, but thus far her eyes were dry and her voice steady. "If you won't tell her, I will. Maybe Barry will hear about it and start wondering how long we've been sleeping together."

"How long have you?" I blurted.

"A couple of months," she said, then leaned against his shoulder and tried to give me a defiant frown. It came across as a pout, but it was infinitely preferable to a deluge. "After the terrible accident that killed Becca, I volunteered to help clean cages. One morning a hawk pooped all over me and I needed to take a shower. Anders decided he did, too."

He smiled at the memory, but I was still too astonished to do more than blink. Other than the embrace in the Dunling Foundation office, I'd seen no evidence that he was sleeping with Agatha Anne. Georgiana was very pretty, conveniently divorced, and an obvious candidate that I'd simply overlooked.

She took a deep breath. "Please don't tell anyone, but I saw the accident, too. I was out in my yard when Agatha Anne came dashing out of her house, and we drove to the marina together. When I got out of the car, I twisted my ankle and had to sit back down in the front seat. I could see the end of the dock, though, and the boat as it sped away . . . and Becca with her golden hair, dressed in a white halter and denim shorts . . . and then . . ." She ran out of breath and looked down.

"I did not know this," Anders said as he put his arms around her. "Why did you not tell me before now?"

"When I realized what I'd seen, I collapsed, sobbing and screaming. Becca was such a dear friend, and she'd been so supportive after the divorce that I . . ." Her voice began to rise and her eyes to glisten, but she swallowed and said, "Agatha Anne said there was no reason for me to be submitted to all the questions—or made to testify if there was an inquest. Bubo hadn't seen me, and she assured me that two witnesses would be enough. She took me home and went back to the marina before the deputies arrived. I crawled into bed and stayed there with the blanket over my head until the next morning. I have nightmares almost every night."

My wonderfully contrived (albeit electronically dubious) beeper theory paled, although it was possible that she'd failed to see someone at the top of the parking lot. "I have one more question," I said. "I can understand why a married woman might insist on a clandestine tryst in town, but you're single. Why did you and Anders meet at Dick's house yesterday afternoon? Why not here or at your house?"

From beneath his sheltering arms she gave me a panicky look, then squeezed her eyes closed and began to speak in a curiously mechanical voice, as if she were a schoolchild mumbling the Pledge of Allegiance. "Last night I dreamed I went to the marina again, but this time I was in the boat with Becca when it exploded. I was flung into the water, and as I tried to swim away from the suffocating black smoke, pieces of her body began to splash down all around me. Her skull bobbled up next to me. It was horrible!"

It was also unresponsive. I looked at Anders, who looked back warily. No one spoke for a long moment.

"About Dick's house?" I finally said.

Georgiana disengaged herself, although she

kept her hand on his thigh, her nails pressing into his flesh. "Anders, go on and tell her how Becca had a key made for you so the two of you could play in Dick's bed while he was at work."

"She found it exhilarating," he said reluctantly. "It was very silly, this need to see how close we could come to being caught, but she thrived on it. I could never say no to Becca, no matter what she was asking."

"You have a house key," I said with an encouraging nod. "Presumably Becca showed you how to disarm the security system if you arrived there before she did, and she showed you how to operate the coffeemaker. That's fine, but it doesn't explain why you two were there yesterday."

Anders sighed. "No, it does not. The reason we were there is very hard to be explaining, I am afraid." He sat back and crossed his arms as if the matter were settled; it was obtuse and therefore unworthy of further discussion.

It was late, and I needed to leave. "I realize it is very hard to be explaining," I said, rudely mimicking his accent, "but why don't you give it a try? No one has accused you of stealing the silver or rifling the safe. I suppose it might be deemed trespassing, but I can assure you Dick will not press charges. He has more important problems."

"We can't tell you right now," said Georgiana. "If you come back this weekend, we can tell you then."

"Why can't you tell me until the weekend?" I

demanded, increasingly frustrated with them. I would have hazarded a guess, but no inspiration came to mind. When neither spoke, I stalked out the door and returned to my car. As I drove up the hill, I heard a blood-curdling cry from the darkness behind the trailer. It captured my mood perfectly.

The following morning I called Luanne at her store to tell her about the encounter and ensuing conversation in the trailer. I went so far as to admit I'd stayed awake well past midnight, staring blindly at a book and searching for an explanation for their behavior.

"I can understand why Becca found it exciting," I said, "but why would they risk Dick or Jillian walking in on them? That wouldn't be exciting—all it would be is embarrassing." I winced as I remembered a night in my teenage years when a policeman had shone a flashlight through a rear window of a car. I'd wanted to crawl into an ashtray and expire. "If they think it's vital to keep their affair a secret from their chums at the lake, then why not go to a motel or her house in town?"

"I guess it'll have to wait until the weekend," she said listlessly, clearly failing to share my enthusiasm for a charmingly elusive problem. "I've arranged for someone to mind the shop for the rest of the week so I can go back to the lake. Sid doesn't think it's politic for Dick to see any patients until this is settled. Oh, and Dick said to tell you he found a private investigator in the Miami area and expects to hear something from him in a few days."

"Have him ask the investigator to see what he can find out about Barry Strix's activities on the day of the accident and this past weekend as well."

"Georgiana's ex-husband?"

"Dick suspected that he and Becca were having an affair. It's likely to have nothing to do with the price of Beluga caviar, but it can't hurt to eliminate him."

"What's the price of Beluga caviar got to do with anything?"

"I just wanted to make sure you were listening."

We talked a while longer. Afterward, I sold a travel guide to an elderly couple, then dragged out my ledger and checkbook and tried to establish a relationship between the two that was not strictly fictional. My ineptitude in such matters reminded me of the Dunling Foundation's problems with its accounting system. Becca had taken over the bookkeeping in December and reduced it to impenetrable chaos in three months. It was painfully true that many more dollars coagulated in their accounts than in mine, but a ledger was still a collection of figures. According to Agatha Anne, Georgiana had a degree in business and the skill with which to manage a medical clinic. It was reasonable to assume she'd inherited her old position after the accident. Why had it taken three months to figure out Becca's eccentric method?

I called my accountant and waited dutifully until he finished lecturing me about my lack of fiscal responsibility and its effect on his digestive processes. I then asked him if there was a book-keeping system that could stymie anyone with a degree and experience.

"Look at your ledgers, Mrs. Malloy," he said peevishly. "Considering all those numbers you scrawl in the margins, those slips of paper with cryptic messages, the illegible invoices, the unrecorded check stubs, I would opine that you have come perilously close to such a system." He grumbled for a moment, then said, "But as long as the figures were not written in a foreign vernacular, I eventually could make sense of them." With a parting grumble, he hung up.

Becca was less and less a paragon of perfection. She'd sponged off the Gordons. She'd had an affair with Barry, and as soon as he left town, begun yet another with Anders. She'd boggled the books and baffled her replacement. And she'd been on the boat at the worst conceivable moment, although I had to concede it had not been her fault.

Dick had offered a reasonable explanation for the damning call to the lake house, and I could understand why he'd erased the message on the machine. It was not the sort of message that should be played by strangers. If he was telling the truth, then someone else had called Becca to report the wounded eagle. As a thought struck, my eyebrows rose and my lips formed a flawless circle. The someone had called Becca's house—rather than the office of the Dunling Foundation.

I picked up a pencil and started a list of where people had been late that afternoon (we amateur sleuths are very big on making lists, as well as timetables and convoluted charts). Dick's long-distance bill seemed to verify his whereabouts. Supposedly Sid had been at his office, wiring unruly teeth. Gannet surely had verified this, too; I did not, however, make a note to call him and inquire. Agatha Anne and Georgiana were at Anders's trailer, which not only meant that none of them could have made the call but regrettably suggested that no one had been in the foundation office to take the call.

Hoping someone was there now, I called said office. Livia answered, and I hurriedly asked my question before she could start enthusing about their Eagle Awareness plans.

"In the office?" she said slowly. "I don't think so. I was escorting a church group from a little town called Maggody. They were particularly eager to view bitterns, I believe it was, and it took several hours before we tracked down one. *Oong-KA-chunk!*"

"Pardon me?"

"The American bittern's distinctive call is audible from over a quarter of a mile away."

It occurred to me that Caron's remark about the contents of Livia's cranium was more accurate than I'd realized. "That's good to know," I said hypocritically. "Was Wharton also with this group?"

"No, I seem to think he was outside in the garden all afternoon." She hesitated, then sighed and said, "The ladies and I were just coming to the end of the trail when we heard a boom. I was irritated because I assumed Wharton had taken a potshot at the groundhog, and he—Wharton, not the groundhog—had promised only the night before that he would not do so when there were visitors on the trails. I felt quite awful when I later learned that what we'd heard was the explosion of the boat."

"Then the Dunling Foundation office was uninhabited," I said glumly. "I suppose whoever wanted to report the wounded eagle tried there, then called Becca at home."

"We always arrange to have the telephone answered. Wharton would have taken the cordless out to the garden. Now that I think about it, Captain Gannet asked that very same question, and Wharton was certain that no one called for at least an hour before the dreadful explosion."

"By the way, how are Agatha Anne and Georgiana coming on the books?" I asked.

"I couldn't say. I wish they'd let Wharton

straighten things out. He may not grasp this mysterious system, either, but he is familiar with the accounts. Until this year, he did all the financial reports that are essential to ensure our nonprofit status."

"Why didn't he do them this year?"

"Agatha Anne said that Becca had assumed responsibility for them. Becca was such a talented young woman, and so very adept at everything she tried. At her request, I taught her how to bake bread, and the next week she brought us a delicious loaf of whole-grain and a jar of homemade raspberry jam. I warned Dick that he'd better watch his waistline." She chuckled at her wit.

I wished her a pleasant afternoon, then wasted the remainder of mine drawing a map of the Blackburn Creek development. The result resembled a serving of spaghetti. I was wondering if I had a jar of tomato sauce in a kitchen cabinet when Luanne called.

"I'm at the lake," she said. "Jillian hasn't returned. No one has seen or heard from her for over twenty-four hours. Dick's been calling the house in town every ten minutes, but there's no answer. Could you please drive by, and if her car is there, make sure she's okay and call us?"

I agreed, locked the store, and drove across town to the opulent neighborhood, entertaining myself with a fantasized scenario in which Anders and Georgiana frolicked under the sheets while Jillian, dressed in black like Anders's beloved *mormor*, stood at the foot of the bed and sternly lectured them in Swedish.

Jillian's car was parked in the garage, but there was no ominous hose attached to the tailpipe. I rang the doorbell, then pounded with my fist. If Jillian was inside, she was not in the mood for company. I jammed the button and pounded for a while longer, then circled the house, peering into windows for a glimpse of her. The interior looked exactly as it had the previous day—elegantly inhospitable.

I returned to the back of the house, where I was less likely to be observed by nosy neighbors. Reminding myself that I was there at Dick's behest, I picked up a rock from a flower bed and smashed the glass pane in the door. I carefully reached through the shards and unlocked the door, then replaced the rock as best I could and entered the kitchen.

"Jillian?" I called. "It's Claire Malloy."

The coffee cup was now in the dishwasher, its rim pristine. The plate on the coffeemaker was cool to the touch. The pizza that had been in the refrigerator was gone, and it seemed as if a few items had been shifted. None of this was newsworthy, since it was obvious that Jillian had returned to the house sometime after the bail hearing. Anyone who'd heard her father accused of two murders might have found solace in pepperoni pizza.

I quickly searched downstairs, then called her

name as I went to the second floor. I was met with resounding silence. Jillian's room showed little evidence of occupancy, but I doubted it ever did. A toothbrush was damp, however, and two sensible shoes were visible under the bed. I heard a quiet hum and tracked it to her computer atop a shoddy student desk. Small greenish lights indicated that parts of the system were running, but the screen was black except for a pulsating oblong no wider than a quarter of an inch at the top of the screen and a row of numbers and letters across the bottom. My understanding of computers was comparable to that of remote-control beepers.

I left the computer to do whatever it was doing and went across the hall. Dick's bedspread had been smoothed. There was no glaring indication that anyone had been in the adjoining bathroom and dressing room. I continued down the hall, opening doors, calling Jillian's name, and growing increasingly nervous. Hide-and-seek is a game best left to children; had I known I'd be forced to participate, I would have told Luanne to call the police. Or called them myself.

Holding my breath, I opened the door to Dick's office. No one leaped out of a corner to confront me. Luanne had mentioned smelling cigarette smoke. Now there was a trace of acridity in the room. I approached the desk, then stopped as the hairs on my neck rose. I looked over my shoulder at the portrait of Becca.

It had been savaged. A blade had crosshatched her face to such a degree that there remained only thin slivers of canvas. Red spray paint obliterated the golden hair and blue gown. The word "Murderer!" had been written in sloppy block letters on the wall beside the painting. The paint can lay on its side by the baseboard.

I stumbled backward, catching the edge of the desk to steady myself. The vandalism was obscene, laden with hate. I forced myself to lean forward far enough to touch a dribble of paint, then gulped as I stared at my fingertip. It looked as if a lab technician had pierced it with a lancet. The stinging sensation was a product of my imagination, but nevertheless vivid. An image of Captain Gannet's smirky face crossed my mind—he would love this.

Abruptly, I wanted to talk to Peter, to let him take charge of the entire mess. It was no longer a scintillating puzzle. It was nasty. Someone was out of control. There was a telephone on the desk—and new additions, I realized. Amid the papers and journals was an amber plastic pill vial, the lid beside it. A glass of water had formed a white circle on the wood veneer.

And on the floor behind the desk was sprawled Jillian Cissel. I dropped to my knees and touched her flaccid hand. She was unconscious, her skin clammy, her breathing shallow and labored. I abandoned any concern for preservation of evidence and called 911. The dispatcher answered immediately, and once I described the scene, told me to cover her with a blanket and wait for the medics.

I found a blanket in the hall closet and did as instructed. Nothing about her demeanor had changed, although mine had taken a turn for the worse. I remembered that the front door was locked, and hurried down to unlock it and leave it ajar. As the seconds crawled by, I felt as though I should be doing something for Jillian. I went into her room to get a pillow, then went over to the computer and frowned at it. The white oblong blipped blithely. The series of characters in the lower right corner of the screen read: *Doc 1 Pg 2 Ln 1" Pos 1"*.

"Document number one, page number two," I said under my breath. "Where's page number one?"

I examined the keyboard, then tentatively pushed the key marked with the numeral one. It appeared in the upper left corner, and I noted a change in the bottom line. We had advanced to *Pos 2"*. The space bar advanced us to *Pos 3"*, and a key marked *Delete* returned us to *Pos 1"* as the numeral vanished. Nothing happened when I tried it again. I looked elsewhere for a key that might take me to the first page of the document, carefully erasing my errors.

A key with an arrow pointing upward sent the cursor racing. I jerked my finger off the key as lines of characters came into view, leaned forward, and read them with a growing dread.

The document read: "On the night of August 29, 1991, my father murdered my mother. He pretended to get drunk at the party, but witnesses said he did not drink excessively. He invited my mother to swim, then held her beneath the water until she was dead. His fingerprints were not on the brandy decanter because he was careful to wipe them off before he handed it to her for the last time. He does not know I saw this from a window in the living room. He did it because he wanted to marry Becca, but then he became obsessed with jealousy and murdered her, too. The morning of her death she told me that he had threatened to kill her and she was afraid. He does not deserve to look at her portrait. I cannot go on. Jillian."

I heard voices below.

An hour later, Luanne and Dick arrived at the emergency room. She sat down beside me while he strode to the nurse's station, conferred briefly, and then went into a curtained cubicle. He emerged seconds later with various medical personnel. A Farberville police officer joined them.

I told Luanne what had happened, adding that the paramedics had begun emergency treatment for barbiturate poisoning in the office. "The sleeping pills," I added, "came from a year-old prescription with Becca's name on it. There's no way to determine how many Jillian took."

"How could she do such a terrible thing?" Luanne said, dazed and pale, her eyes on the group in the corridor, her fingernails biting into her palms. "I should have gone by the house this morning when I got back to town. I knew she was upset, but I had no idea she was this deeply disturbed. To make those wild accusations and destroy the portrait like that and then . . ."

I shivered as I remembered the aura of hatefulness that had pervaded the office as I stared at the portrait. "Something must have caused her to erupt, and a totally different personality took over. We all misjudged her, Luanne. You can't blame yourself for what happened."

She began to cry. I found a tissue in my purse, patted her hand ineffectually, and wished I could overhear what was being said in the corridor. Dick's forehead was lowered and his expression stony. The doctor and nurses returned to the cubicle, and the police officer led Dick around a corner. We sat amid a swirl of nurses and technicians, speeding gurneys, garbled announcements on a PA system, insistent telephones, and members of the walking wounded. A woman with a screaming baby was hurried into a cubicle. A sullen teenage boy with a gash on his cheek was instructed to sit in the waiting room. A frail elderly couple came in and were led through another set of doors. A pasty young woman plied a vending machine, cursing steadily as she fed it change.

Luanne blew her nose and stuffed the tissue in her pocket. "Was there red paint on Jillian's hand?"

"On her right index finger and thumb. There was also a faint dusting on her blouse where the spray had drifted on it." I surreptitiously rubbed my finger against the armrest of the chair. As if in response, the uniformed officer stepped into view, gave me a hard look, and then disappeared. A bad sign, I thought.

This was confirmed shortly thereafter when Lieutenant Peter Rosen came into the emergency room and headed down the corridor. He did not acknowledge my presence, but he would. It was as inevitable as the yearly greeting from Publishers Clearing House.

I mentally re-created one of my lists. Jillian had stayed at the house in town on Saturday night, or had claimed as much. She returned to Turnstone Lake on Sunday afternoon shortly after Dick was arrested. She'd been unnaturally emotional that day—but she'd insisted her father had not murdered Becca. She locked herself in her room the following day. After the bail hearing on Tuesday, she drove away, and she'd not been seen until I'd discovered her a full day later. What had provoked her to change her mind about Becca's death, and why suddenly had she offered the damning testimony about her mother's death?

Her motive for destroying the portrait seemed weak. Jillian might have been oblivious to some of Becca's less enchanting traits, but she certainly had never spoken of her with appreciable warmth or affection. Or with any great animosity, for that matter.

Luanne stood up as Dick came across the waiting room. "How is she?" she demanded.

"Unconscious. Her stomach's been pumped. They've got her on a respirator and an IV. They're worried about kidney failure." He sat down and rubbed his face with both hands. "Why did she leave that message on her computer? I didn't pretend to be drunk that night; I was staggering by the time we got to the house. Is it possible I was so drunk that I don't remember going down to the water with Jan . . . and holding her down? If so, I'm a monster. Jillian must have been driven crazy by the thought she'd inherited some genetic flaw."

"Of course you're not," Luanne said, "and you didn't kill anyone. It was dark and Jillian had taken powerful medicine that made her groggy. She must have seen someone else."

He gave her an agonized look. "If you have any sense, you'll walk out of here and never speak to me again. The women in my life don't fare too well. Except for my mother. She's still alive and healthy, but maybe that's because she lives three states away. God, I'd better call her, and Sid and

Agatha Anne." He went to a pay phone and began to punch buttons.

Peter glanced sharply at him as he stopped in the doorway and issued instructions to the uniformed officer. He crossed the room and said to Luanne, "You can remain here with Cissel, who will be taken into custody if he attempts to leave the hospital. An officer has been assigned to stay with him. When he finishes his call, tell him that his daughter has been moved to IC." To me, he said, "Let's go." It was not an invitation.

"I'd like to stay with Luanne and Dick."

"I'm sure you would, but we're going to the PD. Someone's driven all the way across the county, and he's very eager to talk to you. So am I."

"How lovely to feel needed," I said as I squeezed Luanne's shoulder and followed Peter out the door. The hairs on his neck were bristling in a way I found alluring, but I failed to say so. It would remain to be seen what else I would fail to say to him—or to Captain Gannet. Among my virtues is a good deal of contrariness.

13

I called the hospital before I left the police station after what evolved into a three-hour marathon of questions and demands that I repeat my story forward, backward, and any other conceivable direction. Luanne told me that Jillian remained in critical condition, and hemodialysis had been required. Pneumonia was possible. Dick refused to budge from a chair beside her bed and had not spoken except to refuse coffee or food. She did not want me to come, so I went home.

Lulled by the static from a test pattern on the television screen, Caron slept on the sofa. I smiled at the incongruity of the one-eared teddy bear under her arm and the copy of *Lady Chatterley's Lover* on the floor. I turned off the set and shook her shoulder. "You didn't need to wait up for me. Go on to bed."

"I didn't wait up for you," she said as she sat up and squinted at the dark screen. "I was watching a dirty movie on cable."

"And fell asleep in the middle of it?"

"It wasn't nearly as dirty as Rhonda said it was. No one stuck any dandelions in any pubic hair, and all the full frontal nudity was of the girl. I thought this was the age of sexual equality." She shot me a look meant to imply I was in some way responsible, then said, "I had to use my own money to order a pizza. The delivery boy was a real hunk, but I didn't have enough for a decent tip and he positively sneered at me. I wanted to Lie Down And Die. Where have you been?"

I gave her a synopsis of the previous six hours. "I'll go by the hospital in the morning and see if there's anything I can do."

"Like donate a kidney?"

"Like offer to sit with Jillian while they get some breakfast," I said, reminding myself that my daughter was pink and healthy, if also smart-mouthed and developing an alarming interest in all things pornographic. Dick Cissel's daughter was on a respirator, with needles in her arms, monitors attached to her body, and an ambiguous prognosis.

Caron staggered to the hall, then stopped. "Why did she go buffleheaded and slash the painting and try to kill herself?"

"Nobody knows."

"Then maybe she didn't." Yawning, she retreated to her bedroom.

I was still thinking about Caron's comment as I brushed my teeth and changed into a cotton

nightshirt. Gannet and Peter had been regaled
with every last particle of information that I pos-
sessed (if not every theory I'd toyed with), and
they'd seemed as unable as I to discern the provo-
cation for Jillian's explosive behavior. Gannet
was delighted with the new accusation on Jillian's
computer screen. He had arranged for Anders
and Georgiana to be picked up and held in custody until he could interview them, but gloatingly
had pointed out they'd been in the house the day
before the hearing. It was highly implausible that
they would have returned after I'd confronted
them; they were more apt to be worried about
what I'd told Dick. The truth was that I hadn't
told him anything, but Luanne might have. In any
case, Jillian had been in residence. They would
have had more titillation trying to stay one bed
ahead of the Dunlings.

Outside, the wind rose and thunder rumbled in
the distance. I watched the shadows on the ceiling
for a long while before I fell asleep. For some reason I couldn't define, I kept thinking about how
my science fiction hippie had come into the store
without my knowledge. How long would he have
been a part of the background before I realized he
was there?

Rain fell fitfully as I drove to the hospital at
eight in the morning. Agatha Anne and Sid were
in the IC waiting room when I stepped off the
elevator. She wore a suitably somber skirt and
blouse, and only the essential jewelry. Sid wore

what I supposed was the official pedodontal en-
semble: white trousers, a pink shirt, and a pink-
and-white-striped bow tie. Perhaps the overall
effect was meant to dazzle his patients into submission. I decided he resembled a well-known
diarrhea remedy.

"How's Jillian?" I asked.

"She's still critical," Agatha Anne replied, as-
suming the appropriate "we have a crisis" voice
as well as the attire. "There have been no negative developments, so that's encouraging. Luanne
went down to the cafeteria to get some coffee.
Dick is sitting by Jillian's bed, staring at her."

"Like a zombie," added Sid. He didn't look all
that animated himself, but they'd probably been
at the hospital most of the night. "Now that
Claire's here to keep you company, I'm going
down to the lobby to call the office and have
them start canceling appointments. I need to be
here in case"—he swallowed unhappily—"there's
something I can do for Dick."

Agatha Anne patted my arm as I sat down on
the plastic couch. "It's so lucky that you went to
the house yesterday evening. If the poor girl had
been left undiscovered, she wouldn't have had a
chance." She dabbed away a tear with a mono-
grammed handkerchief. "We've known Jillian
from the day she was born. She's always been so
serious and aloof, and I never suspected she was
capable of—of what she did last night. She adored
Becca, as did all of us. Luanne said the portrait

was desecrated to the point it can't possibly be restored."

"I wouldn't think so," I said. Luanne apparently had briefed them; I waited to see if she would mention the damning message left on the computer screen. She chose a new topic.

"Georgiana came by last night and told me about your visit to Anders's trailer. She said you were absolutely astounded when she walked out of the bedroom. Were you expecting someone else?"

"No," I said firmly, although we both knew precisely whom I'd expected (had I expected anyone, which in all honesty I hadn't). "They promised to explain this weekend why they were in Dick's house Monday afternoon. Captain Gannet's moved up the schedule. They may be in his office at this very moment."

"You told him they were there?" she asked in a low and less friendly tone. "Was that necessary?"

"Captain Gannet arrived at the Farberville PD last night before I did, and I told him quite a lot of things. Anders admitted he had an affair with one of the victims, and he and Georgiana were in the suspect's house earlier this week. It seemed relevant to share this, even though it's out of his jurisdiction."

"He'll be disappointed. Georgiana had this incredibly dumb idea that she could erase Becca's memories from Anders's mind by sort of blurring them with her physical presence. She's not been entirely rational since Barry left, and I couldn't talk her out of it. They were in the master bedroom when they heard a car come up the driveway. Once they saw it was you rather than the postman, they grabbed their clothes and went flying out the back door."

"I hope they don't tell that to Gannet."

She waited until a nurse passed by, then frowned at me as though I were more irrational than Georgiana. "Why not?"

"Because if they saw anybody, it would have been Luanne. She heard the back door close, left immediately, and raced to the bookstore to persuade me to return with her. She's the one who saw Anders's truck as it was driven by the end of the driveway."

"But you told Anders you saw him."

"I lied. I didn't lie to Gannet, though. If he catches me in another one, he'll have me beheaded. A certain lieutenant on the Farberville force might offer to bring the ax and the basket."

"Oh . . ." Agatha Anne searched her mind for what I suspected was the harshest permissible word. ". . . dear."

"Liars seem to be as thick as ticks in a thicket at Turnstone Lake," I continued, hoping she appreciated the alliteration. "For instance, someone lied to Becca about the wounded eagle. Do you remember the wording she used when she left the message on your machine? Did she say anything to imply the gender of the person who made the report, or what he or she was doing at the time?"

"The message was very brief. She said that she'd had a call that an eagle had been shot on Little Pine Island, and she wanted to go there before it got too dark. She reminded me that we were invited for dessert and bridge later."

"I don't suppose you kept the tape?" I asked without optimism. Her recitation had been perfunctory; not even the final invitation evoked emotion. I needed nuances.

"I erased the message as soon as I'd finished listening to it. It's a habit of mine."

The elevator doors opened and Luanne emerged, carrying a raincoat and umbrella. Despite her neatly pressed dress, she looked frumpish and very tired, and the smile she gave me was as perfunctory as Agatha Anne's recounting of the message. She set down a sack from a fast-food restaurant, then went to the IC doors and looked through the glass panel.

"There's been no change," Agatha Anne said. "I thought you were going to the cafeteria."

"I decided to go to my apartment and freshen up," she said. "Dick needs to take a break. I brought coffee and sandwiches, but I don't suppose he'll want anything."

Agatha Anne stood up. "Maybe Sid can convince him when he gets back. If you'll excuse me, I'm going to find a ladies' room and do some freshening up myself." She narrowly averted a collision with an aluminum cart as she went around a corner.

"Do you have the key to the house at the lake?" I asked Luanne.

"Why?"

"There must be some reason why Jillian was so incensed that she did what she did. Maybe she kept a journal. Her bedroom in town is marginally less impersonal than a hotel room, but there were some books and papers in her bedroom at the lake. I want to search it before Gannet thinks to do it himself."

"What if he catches you?"

I shrugged. "I'll tell him Dick sent me to get her bathrobe and personal items. I can be back in less than three hours, and there's no big hurry to open the store. No one ever buys books in the rain. It's a tradition, if not some obscure blue law left over from the previous century. Please lend me the key, Luanne."

She didn't look completely convinced as she took a key from her purse and handed it to me. Our eyes met, and then I left.

The rain worsened as I drove the now familiar route. Lightning periodically shot downward, and the ensuing thunderclaps seemed to buffet my car. The dirt roads were reduced to long, narrow puddles; muddy water cascaded down the hillside and streamed across the road. Not a creature was stirring, and I wondered how the eagles and eaglets were faring. It would be a disaster for the Dunling Foundation if they relocated before the weekend. I could easily picture Livia perched on a branch, holding an umbrella to shelter the aerie.

I encountered no other vehicles. Most of the residents were either at the hospital or at the sheriff's office, and the weather was not conducive to any water sports—with the exception of jumping over puddles. As I paused at the top of the driveway to Dick's house, I glanced at the parking lot in front of Dunling Lodge. The jeep was next to the porch. An unfamiliar car was parked near the beginning of one of the bird trails. Whoever was slogging through the swamp was apt to have quite an adventure.

Rain pelted my face and slithered beneath my collar as I dashed to the front door. Once inside, I paused to catch my breath, then went into the kitchen and used several paper towels to dry myself as best I could. I returned to the living room and looked out the window. The lake was dotted with whitecaps, and there were no overly zealous fishermen in sight. The sky was low, the clouds dark. The hills across the lake were lost in the fierce rain.

Abruptly there was a loud crack. A huge branch crashed onto the deck, its smaller branches obscuring the wicker furniture. Other trees swayed like demonic dancers as the wind beset them. I scanned the sky for a funnel. With the exception of lapsing into hysteria, I wasn't sure what I'd do if I actually saw a tornado bouncing across the lake. I fervently vowed to read up on weather-related emergency tactics as soon as I had a chance. Surely somewhere in the store was a book titled *Tornado Tips* or *How to Host a Hurricane*.

Lightning stabbed the hillside, and I'd counted to one-thousand-and-three when thunder rattled the house. Smaller branches skidded across the deck. A smattering of leaves plastered themselves against the window as if seeking asylum. A thud above me indicated something had fallen on the roof.

I decided to conduct my search and leave before the storm grew any more enthusiastic. I went into Jillian's bedroom and flipped the switch. Nothing happened. I tried the lights in the hall and guest room, then acknowledged gloomily that the power was out.

I had no desire to linger until it was restored. Jillian's room was dim, but not to the degree that I couldn't see. I began with her dresser drawers. When they yielded nothing more interesting than underwear and dark sweaters, I scrupulously put a gown and a pair of socks on the bed before moving on to the bedside table. On the lower shelf were ornithology textbooks; for lighter reading, she'd chosen Daphne du Maurier and Emily Brontë. The drawer contained nasal spray, pencils, and a pair of reading glasses. All the papers concerned Dunling Foundation schedules. I tried the closet, and was finally rewarded with a packet of letters held together with a rubber band.

Sitting on the bed, I slipped off the rubber band and was about to take a letter from an envelope when an unfamiliar female voice drawled, "Reading other people's mail is a sign of poor breeding."

I froze. To my credit, I did not scream, although the idea did cross my mind. It did so at approximately the speed of light.

"You do adhere to the three Bs, don't you?" she went on, her amusement evident. "I've already mentioned breeding. The other two, of course, are brains and beauty."

I turned to look at the woman in the doorway. Her expression was less mesmerizing and her gaze a good deal cooler than in the portrait, but her delicate features and golden hair were unmistakable. She wore shorts, a wrinkled dress shirt that was likely to have come from Dick's closet, and a full-length silvery fur coat. It was not a common combination. "B is also for Becca, I suppose," I managed to say despite the erratic pounding of my heart and constricted throat.

She tilted her head and gave me a sweetly puzzled smile. "You seem to know who I am, but I don't believe we've ever been introduced. May I ask who you are and why you're searching Jillian's room? I suppose B could be for burglar, as improbable as it sounds. You don't look like one, but in this day and age, one cannot be too careful."

My thoughts were chaotic, to describe them charitably. "You were killed in an explosion."

"And now you think I'm a ghost?" Her laugh was lilting and almost contagious, and her eyes seemed to glitter with pleasure. "That is rich, truly rich. I've been accused of many things, but never of having haunted someone. Should I wiggle my fingers in the air and shout, 'Boo!'?"

I shook my head.

"I know what let's do," she said. "Since the power is off, we can't have coffee. Let's have Bloody Marys, shall we? You'll have a marvelous story to tell afterward about how you sipped drinks with a ghost while the wind howled and the storm raged. If I'd had advance notice of your visit, I would have found something diaphanous to wear. What a shame we don't have a camera!"

I left the letters on the bed and followed her into the kitchen. After she assembled the drinks, we went into the living room.

"You still haven't told me who you are," she reminded me as we sat across from each other. She crossed elegantly sleek legs and snuggled her hands into the fur collar that framed her face.

I didn't know how to answer her. Categorizing myself as a friend of her husband's current lover seemed crass, and my breeding had been doubted. "I'm a friend of Jillian's," I said at last.

"And how is she doing?"

I was beginning to get a grip on my thoughts, although they were still a bit chaotic. It was distinctly possible that any marvelous stories I related in the future would feature a cold-blooded killer rather than an ephemeral spirit. "Jillian's doing just fine," I said.

"Is she?" Becca said. "I haven't seen her in months, naturally."

"Months—or yesterday?"

"Wasn't I blown to smithereens three months ago, more or less? I've never known what exactly a smithereen is. Do you have any idea?" She gave me a mildly annoyed look. "I still don't know your name."

"Claire Malloy," I said.

"Ah, yes." She took a gold cigarette case out of her purse and delicately plucked a victim from it. "The famous snoop. You weren't being truthful when you said you were a friend of Jillian's, were you? You're a friend of the woman Dick's been dating these last couple of weeks. You came at her request to try to prove Dick didn't murder poor little me. How are you doing with that?"

"I think we can concede that he didn't murder you. Therefore, all three witnesses lied about seeing you on the boat. One of them is no longer with us."

"Dick did the community a service when he killed Bubo Limpkin. I felt positively itchy every time I went into the marina office to pay for gasoline or purchase a soda. Bubo was an oily little weasel."

"Wait a minute," I said. "Your presence proves Dick didn't murder you. Bubo couldn't have been blackmailing him." I flinched as lightning shot downward. Thunder resounded within a nanosecond. There was something almost comical about the situation: a dark and stormy day, a dimly lit room, an apparition clad in luxurious fur. Almost, but not quite. Otherwise, I certainly wouldn't have been perspiring to the point I was licking salt out of the corners of my mouth.

"Bubo could have been blackmailing Dick for some other reason," she said as she blew out a stream of smoke. Nothing about her was the least bit damp. "My dear husband might be trafficking in Smurf gas, or even more dastardly, shooting eagles. I'd hate to incur the wrath of the Dunling Foundation. I played tennis with Agatha Anne and Georgiana, and I understand Wharton has ordered a flamethrower to incinerate the groundhog."

A gust of wind hurled a branch against the window. I bit back a yelp and tried to verbalize an idea as indistinct as the sky. "You did incur the wrath of the Dunling Foundation," I said slowly. "You took their money, didn't you? You took their money and went—where? Key West?"

"For a month, then I kissed Barry good-bye and went to Paris."

"Leaving Agatha Anne and Georgiana to try to

cover up your theft. It's no wonder they panic whenever someone offers to help decipher the books. I would suggest your accounting system was very straightforward: you converted all the assets to cash and wrote yourself a big check. The Dunling Foundation will be ruined if it's known that all those donations went to fund your trip to Paris."

"Birds have survived for one hundred and forty million years without the aid of the Dunling Foundation," Becca said dryly. "Somehow or other, they managed to get by without brochures to illustrate their migratory paths and mating behaviors. At some point a caveman might have donned a T-shirt with an ecologically correct motto and taken his tribe on a bird walk, but in general, the birds have done just fine."

I wasn't ready to be drawn into a debate about the usefulness of the foundation. "On the day of the so-called accident, you went to the office and wrote the check. How did you get into town?"

"Anders offered me a lift."

"And took you to the airport?"

"I do prefer to fly, but I was a teensy bit worried that the police might make inquiries at the Farberville airport, and even at the bus station. Anders was sweet enough to drive me to a town fifty miles away, where I put on a boring brown wig and sunglasses and climbed onto a bus. Buses smell dreadful, don't they?"

I went into the kitchen to replenish our drinks

while I thought this over. "When Anders arrived at his trailer," I said as I came back into the living room, "he was met by two very unhappy members of the foundation. They decided the only way to cover up your disappearance was to fake the explosion in the boat. Your body would be lost at sea, so to speak, and they would receive the insurance money to cover expenses until the next fund-raiser. Bubo would have readily accepted a bribe. I'm surprised Anders went along with it."

Her expression reminded me of the red-tailed hawk. "Anders had way too many shots of vodka one night and told me a fascinating story. It seems he got into some trouble twenty or so years ago while he was studying in New York and felt the need to disappear. He lacks one of those cute little green cards, and he worries that the immigration authorities are interested in his whereabouts."

"Does Agatha Anne know this?"

"Of course she does, as does Georgiana. We were dear, dear friends, you know. I let it slip while we were having lunch. It turned out to be useful to all three of us to have something to dangle over his gorgeous blond head."

"What about Jillian? Was she part of the conspiracy?"

"I don't know, Claire. Bear in mind that I was *not* part of it. While they were blowing up the boat, I was on a bus ride to an adjoining state, and a day later on a flight to Key West. I rather expected them to file charges and unleash blood-hounds to hunt me down. I had no inkling I was dead until Barry called Sid at my request to find out what was happening. Barry reported that Sid sounded very depressed when he described my fatal accident. Sid is such a dear, isn't he?"

"So is Dick, You spotted him immediately as the most likely nominee for your husband, didn't you? There was only one small hindrance—his wife. By sheer coincidence, she died within a matter of months. Dick was overwhelmed, and it was fortunate that you were there to ease him out of his grief and eventually assume the role of the second Mrs. Cissel. Then you grew tired of that, and went away to become the second Mrs. Strix."

"Heavens no," she said, wrinkling her nose. "Barry was too enamored of his freedom to be trusted. Fidelity is so vital to an enduring relationship. Besides, I needed Barry only long enough to do some little banking chores and book a flight to Paris. Paris is truly divine in April." She lit another cigarette and sighed dreamily. "I had a lovely, lovely time with Jean Paul, and then with Enrico, who's an Italian count and an infamous scoundrel. He's no longer allowed in the casinos at Monte." She arched her eyebrows at me. "I mean Monte Carlo, naturally. Have you ever been there?"

"And then the money ran out?" I suggested as I went to the window and looked out at the lake. The rain had slackened to a mist, but the whitecaps seemed to race across the water like tiny sailboats. The sky was no less gray. I opened the sliding glass door and stepped over the dripping foliage. "Why did you come back to Farberville? Weren't you worried that someone would spot you and you'd end up in jail?"

"Very much," she said as she joined me, "but I was desperate for money and I kept thinking about the jewelry I'd left in the safe in Dick's office. I'd intended to pick it up on my way out of town, but Dick's car was in the driveway. I couldn't risk a confrontation with him that would delay my departure. If Georgiana had opened the foundation checkbook and then conferred with the bank, she would waste no time calling the police."

It occurred to me that I might call the sheriff's office, if the telephone lines weren't down. I was about to concoct an excuse to go inside when Becca said, "There's where poor Jan left her clothes the night she took her last swim. She was a wonderful woman, quiet and unassuming, but with a sly sense of humor that needed a little coaxing. I cried all day after her body was found. We'd planned to have lunch and go shopping."

"Jillian accused Dick of drowning her mother. It's absurd, and I'm sure she'll have an explanation when she recovers. In her original statement, she claimed to have slept soundly until Dick roused her."

"If she recovers."

Mendacity was in order. "She was doing much

better when I left the hospital this morning. She's off the respirator and is expected to regain consciousness during the day." I gave her a chance to feign surprise that Jillian was in the hospital at all, but she was frowning—and very possibly grinding her perfectly capped teeth. "I don't know what she'll remember about last night. What she won't remember is destroying the portrait and typing a suicide note on her computer. You did those after you drugged her and left her to die, didn't you?"

"I don't appreciate your remarks, Claire. I believe it's time for me to leave."

I tried not to gasp as I saw Livia Dunling come out onto the patio of the lodge. The binoculars hung around her neck, but she appeared more interested in inspecting the bird feeders for damage from the storm. "Why did you come here in the first place?" I said, stalling as I willed Livia to aim the binoculars at the deck. "No, let me guess. You were staying at the house in town, but decided that wouldn't work after Jillian's body was discovered. Dick would stay in town, no matter what the outcome of your attempted murder." I began to gesture broadly at her, hoping that a crude imitation of a bird might catch Livia's attention. "Did I interrupt you last night while you were trying to get into the safe? Did Luanne frighten you away Monday afternoon when she went to pick up the mail? Did Jillian walk in and surprise you Saturday night?"

She gave me a bewildered look. "I don't think you'd better have anything more to drink, Claire. I unexpectedly encountered Jillian at the house on Saturday, as you said. I hadn't planned on her return Tuesday evening, but there she was. It was her home. I couldn't refuse to allow her to stay there, could I? Then she became petulant when I asked if she knew where her father kept the slip of paper with the combination to the safe. I'd tried every sequence of birth dates, addresses, and telephone numbers."

"So you doped her," I said. I resisted the urge to climb onto the rail and screech like an eagle. I took a quick peek at the patio of the lodge and lowered my arms. Livia Dunling was no longer visible.

Becca stepped inside, then returned to stand in the doorway. "I'm sorry to have to end our conversation this way," she said as she pointed a gun at me. "You're a dear to be so worried about Dick and Jillian. I appreciate that kind of concern and generosity."

"Jillian will tell the police everything."

"I suppose so, but I'll be long gone. In his haste to get to the hospital, Dick left behind his wallet filled with gold and platinum cards. I know someone in Miami who will pay a decent price for them. Not enough for Paris, I'm sorry to say, but enough to keep me going until I make new friends."

Abruptly she went sprawling into the mess of

sodden leaves and branches. The gun continued over the rail. She began to tussle like a wounded groundhog, her furry rump wriggling as she struggled to disentangle herself.

Agatha Anne stepped onto the deck.

14

Becca extricated herself with a few choice phrases that were hardly droplets of honey. She brushed leaves off her coat, then turned around and held out her arms to her assailant. They made chirpy noises as they kissed the air above each other's cheeks.

"Agatha Anne, you look wonderful!" burbled Becca. "Have you done something new with your hair—or have I simply forgotten how attractive it is?"

"I had Roberto take off an inch," she replied, unable to keep herself from twirling a lock around her finger. "But yours looks fantastic! Surely I'm not imagining just a hint of frosting?"

Becca took Agatha Anne's arm and led her to the settee, which was the only piece of furniture not under several feet of horizontal oak. "I found this genius in Paris. He was mad for me, of course, and I used to torment him by threatening to have my hair done elsewhere. Let me give you his number. You'll have to make an appointment six months in advance."

I'd have felt more comfortable if I'd been dropped into a DAR meeting. Agatha Anne seemed uninterested in bringing up the obvious topics—the Dunling Foundation's assets—and Becca was praising the virtues of her Parisian hairdresser. In the meantime, Jillian was in a coma at the hospital and Captain Gannet was considering the wording of an arrest warrant.

"If you'll excuse me . . ." I murmured as I started for the doorway into the house.

Agatha Anne broke off her string of compliments. She took a small gun from her purse and pointed it at me. "I wish you wouldn't leave just now."

I scowled at her. "Well, I wish people would stop pointing guns at me. Guns make me very nervous, as do people who pull them out of their pockets and purses. With the exception of insurance fraud, you haven't committed any crimes that I'm aware of. Becca, on the other hand, tried to murder Jillian and frame Dick. We didn't have time to discuss Jan's death, but I wouldn't be surprised to learn she was the one who wiped the decanter and held down the head." I balefully eyed the end of the barrel, which was wobbling but still aimed at my midsection. "You do object to murder, don't you?"

"Of course I do," she said indignantly. "I'm an Episcopalian. But don't you realize that we have eagles nesting at Turnstone Lake for the first time in a century? The Dunling Foundation will be known nationally. I took a call yesterday from a radio station in Chicago that wants to do an interview with me for National Public Radio. Anders has already sold photographs to numerous newspapers and magazines. Donations come in the máil every day. Livia says the aerie will be the pinnacle of her memoirs. You can't spoil all this just because Becca . . . borrowed a few dollars."

"And gave a young woman what may be a lethal dose of barbiturates," I said stonily. "Will your radio interview go quite as well if you've been to Jillian's funeral earlier in the afternoon?"

Agatha Anne turned to Becca, who was picking at her fingernails. "You didn't mean to do anything more than knock her out, did you?"

"Heavens, no. She's like a kid sister to me. If I thought for a minute that she would suffer any serious damage, you know perfectly well I wouldn't have put one single little pill in her coffee. I was thinking I might take her with me the next time I go to Paris. I found a boutique with the most divine things, and the prices are not at all as outrageous as at most of the shops. Oh, and I must tell you about the *parfumerie* I discovered by the Opéra!"

"Would you like to guess which organization funded the shopping spree?" I said to Agatha Anne. "Let's discuss finances. Bubo could not have blackmailed Dick. He was much more likely to blackmail the person who'd paid him to lie about the explosion. What was the going rate?"

"He agreed to swear he'd seen Becca on the boat for a thousand dollars," she said with a dainty shrug. "Ironically, that was exactly how much was left in the Dunling Foundation account."

"And the explosion itself?"

"I turned on the propane and lit a candle in the galley. The boat was aimed at the middle of the lake. As soon as the propane reached a certain level . . ."

"The boat blew up," Becca said admiringly. "I wish I knew more about explosives. They seem so efficient when one needs to dispose of evidence."

"Or lack of evidence," I said. "I'm impressed with your expertise, Agatha Anne."

"Anders suggested the technique. He had some training in that area while he was in college in New York. He joined some radical organization that met in basements."

Becca giggled. "He said it was *de rigueur* for the women to go braless and refuse to shave. As a European, he was accustomed to it. Oh, Agatha Anne, can you imagine the look on Sid's face if he found a patch of wiry hair under your arm? Wouldn't he just die!"

"Could we discuss the marina?" I said with

some desperation. Either one of them was capable of suggesting we reconvene in a restaurant, where we could discuss explosives and blackmail over shrimp salad and white wine. We could discuss the murders while we shopped.

Agatha Anne set the gun down, although in a spot where Becca could not get to it easily. "If you insist. Bubo called me and said that you claimed to be an insurance investigator. He wasn't sure who you were, but he was alarmed and demanded ten thousand dollars that night. It was a Saturday. He refused to listen when I pointed out that banks are closed on Saturdays and I had no earthly way to get that much money. He was mulish and unreasonable. I was prepared to tell him so when I arrived at the marina, but then you came creeping along and I was forced to hide under the captain's chair on our boat. When I got home, I found a live spider in my hair!"

"You poor thing," Becca said, taking her hand. "I remember how much you dislike spiders."

"Was Bubo already dead when you arrived?" I asked.

Agatha Anne looked up at me. "I never saw him, so I have no idea. I hope you're not implying I killed him. I went down to try to convince him that he would find himself in trouble if he switched his story. He'd accepted a bribe and lied to Captain Gannet. At the very least, he would be an accessory to insurance fraud."

Becca took an emery board out of a furry recess and began to file her talons. "Don't bother to ask me, Claire. It did not occur to me to call Bubo when I arrived back in Farberville. All I wanted to do was gather up the jewelry and fade away. It's *très amusant* to be dead. No tax returns, no junk mail, no telephone solicitors. All in all, I strongly recommend it."

Ignoring her was easier by the minute. To Agatha Anne, I said, "Precisely what did you do Saturday night when you arrived at the Blackburn Creek Marina?"

"Georgiana and I decided that I had to at least speak to Bubo. She stayed at the foundation office in case Sid or anyone else called, prepared to cover for me. I walked to the marina and was about to go inside when I saw the headlights on the hill. It would have been awkward to explain my presence, so I hid on my boat. You came down the dock and crouched on the barge in the next slip. It was all I could do not to start giggling when you began to snore. I was about to sneak away when you stood up and went to the end of the dock."

"Did you push me?"

"Yes, but I had no choice," she said, attempting to sound contrite. I was not touched. "There I'd been for what felt like hours, my knees aching, my sinuses dripping from the night air. I had no way of knowing if you might return to the barge and stay there the rest of the night, and I simply couldn't bear another minute on the boat. You're so accomplished in other areas that I was certain you were an excellent swimmer."

"And you saw no one else at the marina?" I persisted. Behind me in the house I heard a door open. It was possible Livia Dunling had seen us on the deck and alerted the sheriff's office. As much as I dislike fictional heroines being rescued by the Mounties, I would have kissed a Mountie and his horse, too. "Are you positive you didn't see anyone?" I said more loudly to let the deputies know where we were. "Did you take the gun that's right there next to you on the end table to the marina?"

"She was acting very peculiar earlier," Becca whispered to Agatha Anne. Her eyes widened as she looked past me into the living room. "We seem to—to have a visitor."

I turned around and prepared to welcome the Mounties, or in this case, Captain Gannet.

Wharton Dunling came across the room and aimed his shotgun at Agatha Anne. "Throw the gun off the deck," he snapped.

"Why, Wharton," she said, stunned, "we're so glad to see you—"

"Throw the gun off the deck." He waited until she had obeyed, then grabbed my arm. "All three of you, let's go."

Becca tried to give him her warmest smile. It was not her best effort to date, but she was doing better than I. "How is Livia? I was so worried about her when she had that heart attack two years ago. I do hope—"

"On your feet," he said. His fingers dug into my arm with surprising strength. "Don't try anything, Mrs. Malloy. You've caused enough trouble already."

For the second time that morning, I was profoundly inarticulate. "I have?"

He gestured for us to precede him. In single file we trooped through the living room and out to the parking lot. It must have been a bizarre sight— Agatha Anne leading in her solemn skirt, Becca in a majestic fur, and I in my utilitarian shirt and jeans. It presented a splendid opportunity for someone to drive up and appreciate the array of lifestyles. No one did.

"In the car," he said, pointing at my hatchback.

Agatha Anne waggled her finger. "It'll be much too crowded, Wharton. Why don't I take my car and follow the rest of you?" He aimed the shotgun at her face. "Or maybe not," she added. "We can manage to squeeze in somehow. May I ask where we're going? I promised Luanne I'd bring her some iced tea and a sandwich at noon. Dick hasn't eaten a thing—"

"Get in the car," Wharton growled. "We're going to the marina."

I was the designated driver. Agatha Anne sat beside me; Becca and Wharton sat in back. The barrel of the shotgun dug into my neck as I drove to the top of the driveway and then hesitated, wishing I had my map. I'd made so many wrong turns that I anticipated them, but Wharton might become irritated. I did not wish to be the source of his irritation.

"Turn right," Agatha Anne said softly.

I took her advice at the ensuing crossroads, and we arrived at the marina without incident. The truck was parked where I'd seen it earlier. There were no other vehicles, no doubt partly because of the signs that proclaimed the marina off-limits and discouraged trespassing with threats of prosecution. The storm was an added inducement.

He ordered us out of the car, then herded us toward the covered dock. I frowned as we passed the barge where I'd hidden. Agatha Anne had pushed me into the lake to avoid an "awkward" explanation. It had led to my awkward encounter with Bubo's body. I vowed to discuss priorities with her at a more propitious moment.

"Exactly what do you have in mind?" Becca asked thoughtfully as we halted at the Gallinagos' boat. "I read an account of my fatal accident, and ever since then I've avoided boat rides. The very thought makes me queasy."

"Get on the boat," he said.

"Now, Wharton," said Agatha Anne, "you need to reconsider this. Livia's heart is not strong. She truly needs someone to take care of her. Left alone, she might wander into the woods and never be seen again."

He repeated his order. Like an orderly troop

of Girl Scouts, we climbed into the boat and waited mutely while he did the same.

A chilly wind began to blow as I watched him take a coil of wire from his coat pocket. It felt like sleet as he removed a candle and set it aside. At his command we sat in a row on a bench. He quickly bound our wrists with wire and knelt in front of Agatha Anne to secure her ankles. The only sound throughout this was rain pelting the metal roof above us.

Time seemed of the essence. "You won't get away with this," I said, frowning at my wrists.

"Why not?" he asked as he moved to Becca's ankles. He sat back and looked up at her. "No one's going to miss this one. She's already dead. As for you two, maybe I'll tell Gannet there was a message on the office answering machine in which you said you were going out together to make sure the aerie survived the storm. Gannet won't be pleased with another mysterious explosion, but there's not much he can do about it."

"Anders and Georgiana know that Becca's not dead," I said, struggling to reason with him as he wired my ankles together. "And Jillian will—"

He yanked the wire tighter. "Jillian won't do anything. Sid called to tell us she passed away two hours ago. From what I heard while you were talking on the deck, that's pretty Miss Becca's fault. That gives me two good reasons to make sure she's on the boat this time."

"It was an error," Becca said promptly. "I either misjudged the dosage or she was overly sensitive. I wouldn't dream of harming such a sweet young woman. It's really rather unkind of you to accuse me of something so terrible, Wharton."

He sat down across from us and gave her an evil smile. "Is embezzling all the money in the Dunling Foundation less terrible? You never bothered to butter me up the way you did the others, maybe because you think I'm nothing but a crazy old coot. I'm not so crazy that I didn't have a look at the accounts and make a few calls to the bank and investment firm. I had an idea where you'd gone, and I made a call to an old army buddy who was a sniper. It's a damn shame you had time to fly the coop." He looked at Agatha Anne. "She wouldn't have if you hadn't tried to cover up her crime to protect your precious reputation. Every time your picture's in the newspaper, you make sure you're identified as the president of the Dunling Foundation. You care more about the society page than you do about the birds, don't you?"

"Don't be absurd," she said with a shaky laugh. "I was worried that Livia might find out. The foundation means so much to her."

He shook his head. "If you'd told me that day, I'd have tracked her down before she spent all the money. I was in the military for thirty years. I have friends in every corner of the country. We could have found her in a matter of days."

I cleared my throat. "Please note that I had

nothing to do with any of this. I'd never met any of you or evinced any great interest in birds. All I did was try to prove Dick's innocence."

"So he can marry your friend," Wharton said, nodding. "This way Dick won't have to bother with a divorce, will he? I'm helping him just like you, Mrs. Malloy. We're on the same team in a way. Teamwork's vital in the military."

"I think you're missing my point," I said. "I'm not responsible for anything that's happened. I can understand your problems with Agatha Anne and Becca, but—"

Despite the wire around her wrist, Becca managed to jab me. "Could you try a different tactic, please?"

Wharton picked up the candle. "I did not miss your point. You have a reputation for meddling. This time you meddled when you should have stayed at home and minded your own business. Agatha Anne and Becca betrayed the Dunling Foundation. There is only one way to deal with traitors. You may consider yourself to be a spy. Spies are dealt with in the same manner." He disappeared into the cabin.

Agatha Anne frowned at her wrists. "This is not going well. Sid is very fond of his boat, and has invited some old friends to fish this weekend. Do either of you have a suggestion?"

Neither of us had offered one when Wharton returned. He turned on the engine, maneuvered the boat out of the slip, and stopped at the end of the dock. Once he'd adjusted the wheel, he stepped out of the boat and pushed the throttle.

"*Bon voyage*," he called as the boat chugged away from the marina.

"How long does it take for the propane to accumulate?" I shouted over the sound of the engine. I stuck my wrists at Becca. "See if you can catch the end."

"And break a nail?"

"It depends," Agatha Anne shouted, "on the rate of escape, obviously." She began to gnaw at the wire with her teeth.

I looked back at the marina. Wharton stood watching us, the shotgun resting in one arm. "As soon as we're out of range, we'll have to jump. I'd rather sink than be incinerated in an explosion. I presume we all know how to swim?"

"I've never tried under these circumstances," Agatha Anne shouted hoarsely.

"Nor have I," Becca said. She'd not raised her voice, but her words were audible.

I struggled to my feet and hopped toward the stern of the boat. I had no idea about the range of the shotgun, but Wharton looked quite small and the distance daunting. "After the boat explodes, find something to hang on to," I said as I looked at the cold, choppy water. "The explosion will bring other people to the marina. We'll be safe."

Agatha Anne and Becca clung to each other as they hopped to my side. The boat lurched, sending us sprawling onto the deck, and it took several precious minutes to struggle back up.

"We'd better jump," I shouted.

Becca leaned forward to look down at the inhospitable water. "I have a slight problem."

"A slight problem?"

"I grew up in a housing project, so I'm not an accomplished swimmer. My coat is likely to drag me down. I think I shall take my chances here on the boat. Wharton may have overestimated the time required for the propane to fill the cabin, or the candle might have gone out. We're nearly halfway across the lake already. In another five minutes, the boat will run into the shore."

I opened my mouth to tell her she had to jump, then realized she was making sense. Her coat would soak up water, and there was no way to remove it. It was unlikely Wharton had much experience in this particular arena. Agatha Anne and I could be in the process of drowning when the boat gently bumped the far side of the lake.

"I smell propane!" screamed Agatha Anne.

Becca pushed me. I had a second to gulp in a breath as I tumbled over the side. Having taken this sort of dive only a few days earlier, I anticipated the coldness of the water. As soon as I stopped plunging downward, I kicked my way to the surface. Agatha Anne's head appeared seconds later, her eyes round and her expression dazed.

The boat was receding. Becca stood at the

helm, her perfect blond hair streaming in the wind.

The boat exploded in a ball of flames and black, roiling smoke.

15

I coughed and gagged as smoke swept over me. Waves slammed into my face. Bits of burning debris bobbled by like miniature funeral barges. My head throbbed with the sound of the explosion. I tried not to think about Georgiana's dream, which had been fabricated especially for me. All things considered, I was not in the mood to swim with a skull.

"Agatha Anne!" I called raggedly, scanning the water. I heard a faint response and moved toward it, but every inch of progress required a great deal of squirming. My hands were useless. I doubted we could make it all the way back to the marina. Exhaustion would drag us down as surely as Becca's fur would have dragged her down. I twisted my head and looked where the boat had been, then resumed my eel-like squirms. There was no hope she had survived.

"Claire?" Agatha Anne called. "Are you okay?"

I refused to waste my breath on a caustic

answer, and arrived at her side. "We need to find something to hold us up," I said. "I don't suppose you've spotted a life preserver?"

"If I had, I'd be hanging on to it, wouldn't I? Do you think a boat will come to investigate?"

"I think we'd better start swimming."

A charred paddle floated into range. It provided only a little buoyancy, but it was not the time to be picky. We discovered our best mode was on our backs. Waves splashed into my eyes and nose, erratically but insistently. Conversation was impossible. I was afraid to look at the dock. If the distance had not lessened appreciably, even the Energizer Bunny would not have been able to keep on going. His little pink self would be at the bottom of Turnstone Lake.

"I can't make it any farther," Agatha Anne said as she clung to the paddle. Her heretofore flawless face was splotched and her hair hung in her eyes. "It's too cold."

I let my feet sink so that I was vertical, a much better position from which to lecture her. "Yes, you can, dammit! We both can. Wharton Dunling is not going to get away with this. We are going to make it to the marina and call for help." I allowed myself a glimpse at our destination and tried to imbue my voice with optimism. "We're halfway there. It's not that far now."

"My entire body is anesthetized from the cold. My ankles are getting puffy and the wire hurts dreadfully."

I raised my hands out of the water long enough to point my finger at her. "This is not the time to start whining."

Her lower lip shot out. "I hate it when my ankles get puffy."

"Let's go," I said, then lay back like a sodden log and began to kick. Her pouty expression had reminded me of Caron, and my stomach churned as I considered the reality that my daughter might be an orphan before she had a driver's license. Tears began to dribble out of the corners of my eyes to be washed away by waves. Nearby I could hear Agatha Anne's snuffles. I squeezed my eyes as tightly as I could and imagined Wharton Dunling's face. It was behind bars.

Periodically, we paused to rest and took turns with the paddle. Agatha Anne's expression remained mutinous, as if I were punishing her for a missed curfew or a bad grade. I wasn't predisposed to defend myself. The distance was dwindling, but there were obvious reasons why swimming while trussed was not an Olympic event.

I finally felt something brush against my foot as we entered shallower water. I was much too depleted to worry about snakes or alligators, or even corpses. The dock was closer. No one had appeared in response to the explosion, but it had taken place in the middle of the lake.

We wiggled our way past the dock and arrived at the boat ramp. Allowing the paddle to drift away, we sat on the concrete and let relief rather than waves wash over us. I looked back at the smoking rubble, but I couldn't judge the distance with any accuracy. It didn't matter how far it was. It had felt like a million miles.

"Shall we call someone?" said Agatha Anne.

"I can't drive the car like this." I made it to my feet and looked at the screen door of the marina office. The lengthy immersion had caused my ankles to swell, and I could barely move my feet. I started up the ramp, one torturous hop at a time.

"My legs are too tired," Agatha Anne said. She began to pick at the wire around her ankles.

It was tempting to rejoin her, but I was worried about Wharton's whereabouts. I continued slowly to the screen door. Yellow tape forbade entry. I ripped it off and opened the door, then held my breath while I turned the knob of the sturdier wooden door. Whoever had put up the tape had found it sufficient warning.

I crumpled into the nearest chair, where less than a week earlier I'd pretended to be an insurance investigator. Had my presence been a catalyst? I decided it had not. Bubo had implied he was preparing to demand a blackmail payoff. My unsuccessful Machiavellian ploy might have affected his agenda, but he would have made the call sooner or later. On a day when banks were open, perhaps.

Clearly, the catalyst was Becca. She had manipulated the events from the moment she swooped in like a vulture to help Marilyn Gordon with her luggage in the Miami airport. She'd orchestrated everything and everybody. She hadn't given Jillian Cissel an overdose because I'd started poking into the accident. She'd done it because it suited her to remain in the background. As Livia had said, Becca had many talents. Baking bread was the least of them.

I hopped to the cash register. My fingers were stiff, and it took effort to scoop out a few coins. I hopped to the pay telephone and told the operator to put me through to the sheriff's office. After I had described the situation to a skeptical dispatcher, I hopped back to the counter and searched through junk-filled drawers for a tool with which to cut the wire. Everything I did was laborious and clumsy; I was deeply gratified that there was no one with a camcorder.

When Agatha Anne came hopping inside, I was sitting at the table, the fillet knife in front of me. My ankles were free, but there'd been no way to cut the wire around my wrists. My hands were on the table in the classic pose of supplication.

"Nice of you to drop in," I said.

"I told you my legs were tired," she said huffily.

We freed each other, then sat back to massage our skin and wait. This time the Mounties really were coming.

Agatha Anne peered at the darkness though the doorway. "Did you make sure Wharton's not in the back room?"

"Why don't you poke your head in there and see for yourself?"

"You're the one with all the experience in this sort of thing. We could be sitting ducks, you know."

"Shut up, bufflehead." My countenance and tone of voice were adequate to elicit her compliance. I took the pilfered change and bought a soda. I did not offer her one. Someday when this was all a vague memory, I would proffer a silent apology to Emily Post, but at the moment I was all out of social graces. "Did you search the back room the night you pushed me in the lake?" I demanded.

"I've already apologized for that, Claire. I had no idea the water was so cold. I certainly wouldn't have pushed you into it if I'd known." She gazed at the harsh white lines around her wrist, as if trying to think which bracelets might best cover them.

"Did you search the back room?"

"No, but whoever did was looking for a cassette of a conversation I had with Bubo the day after the accident. He secretly recorded it."

"It was not an accident," I said sternly.

"You're in a foul temper, aren't you? Anyway, Bubo called me on the telephone and talked about . . . what we did. He emphasized the size of the payment and made sure I acknowledged having made it. When he called me last week, he threatened to mail the cassette to Gannet."

"He called you at home?"

"At the Dunling Foundation office," she said, wistfully eyeing my can of soda. She was much too proper to ask for a sip. Because of my foul (or was it fowl?) temper, I didn't offer her one.

Shortly thereafter Captain Gannet stomped into the office, accompanied by a few familiar deputies. He frowned at me. "You should find a new hairstyle, Mrs. Malloy. This one's not flattering."

"Next time I'm in Paris I'll do just that." I related everything that had happened, overriding Agatha Anne's attempts to interrupt.

Captain Gannet thought it all over for a few minutes, scratching his head and grumbling to himself. "Why did you take a gun to Cissel's house?" he barked at Agatha Anne. "Were you going to shoot the meddlesome Mrs. Malloy?"

She cringed as he glowered at her. "Of course not. I was sitting in the waiting room at the hospital, and all of a sudden I realized that Becca was back. I didn't think she'd done that terrible thing to Jillian, though. I thought maybe she'd convinced Jillian that Dick had murdered her mother, which would explain why Jillian tried to kill herself. I knew Becca couldn't stay at the house in town. It seemed likely that she was hiding at Dick's lake house."

"So you went there to shoot her?" Gannet said.

"Absolutely not! She was a dear friend and I admired her greatly. She had a fantastic backhand, Captain Gannet. I wish you could have seen it yourself. I just thought I'd ask about the money, and if she wasn't cooperative, frighten her a bit." Agatha Anne smiled modestly at the brilliance of her plan.

"Did Luanne tell you I'd taken the key?" I asked.

"No, I don't seem to recall that she did."

"Luanne's judgment may be suspect, but her memory's just fine. We can call her and ask, you know."

"Well, she may have mentioned it," Agatha Anne said. "We didn't really discuss it at any length. I assumed your reasoning had been similar to mine and you suspected Becca was at the lake house."

Captain Gannet met my gaze as he lit a cigarette, then flicked the match on the floor. We both knew Agatha Anne had found an explanation from which she would never budge. "Did Wharton Dunling kill Bubo?" he asked me. I could see from his expression that the necessity to pose the question was having a deleterious effect on his internal organs. It gave a whole new meaning to the word "galling."

"Yes, I think he did," I said. Had I not been sopping wet, I might have basked in the glow of his discomfort. "He eavesdropped on telephone conversations. He must have heard Bubo's demand and decided to take out yet another traitor to the cause. Agatha Anne had no means to get ten thousand dollars, and Bubo was capable of mailing the tape from another state. The Dunling Foundation would be finished. Livia might have a fatal heart attack. He's devoted to her." I shot a dark look at Agatha Anne. "And unlike certain other people, she may well be worthy of it. She honestly is more concerned with the bird sanctuary than with the society page. She grows milkweed for the butterflies, for pity's sake."

"I have a trumpet vine for the hummingbirds," she retorted.

Gannet intervened before I could launch into a diatribe about hypocrisy and other less gracious traits. "I sent a deputy to Dunling Lodge. No one is there, and the jeep is gone."

"Wharton mentioned a nationwide network of vets," I said. "It must have taken us an hour to swim back here and call. He and Livia may be in the next state by now. I wouldn't be surprised if various links in the network have access to false documents." I stopped to think, then added, "You might try the Mexican customs authorities."

"Why would I do that, Mrs. Malloy?" Gannet said with the widest smirk I'd seen thus far. It stretched from ear to ear, and he bore a disturbing resemblance to the Cheshire Cat.

I could not make him vanish, alas, but I could

wipe away his smirk. "That's where the monarch butterflies go when it starts getting cool. In Wharton's case, it's downright cold these days."

He had the grace to blink.

Caron had no grace at all when I related all of this later that afternoon. "What about my job?" she howled. "What about the hundred and seventy-eight dollars for driver's ed?"

"You'll have to find another job," I said.

"Nobody's going to pay ten dollars an hour." She sat down on the floor and flopped against the self-help books. "Dishwashers start at minimum wage and get like a ten-cent raise every year if they haven't broken any dishes."

Inez peeked around the corner of the fiction rack. "I forgot to tell you that Louis Wilderberry's sister called me this morning," she said hesitantly.

"So?"

"They found a sub for Coach Scoter."

"So?"

"It's this retired nun named Louisa Ferncliff. I didn't know nuns retired. I thought they just died. Then again, I thought they were all named Sister something or other."

"Send me to the swamp!" Caron buried her face in her hands. "In North Carolina or someplace stupid like that, there's the Great Dismal Swamp. Maybe they need a facilitator."

I remembered how I'd felt when I doubted I would make it to shore. "I'll make you a deal, dear. We'll forget about driver's ed. You work here without pay and I'll apply the credit toward the difference in the insurance rates. Twelve hours a month, okay?"

"And I take the driver's exam in August?" Caron said, recovering nicely.

"No car, though. You'll have to share mine."

She stood up and gave me a haughty look. "I'll be the laughingstock of the entire high school when I show up in the parking lot. Can't you trade it in for something less nerdy?" When I shook my head, she headed for the door. "Let's ask your mom to take us to the mall, Inez. I want to get that black bikini for Rhonda's party on Saturday. Then I may just call Rhonda and tell her Everything Else that Allison Wade said about her buttocks, not to mention her thighs."

The bell jangled, and then I was alone. It was raining, which meant the sidewalks were empty and the traffic sparse. I anticipated no customers. In two more years Caron would leave for college (little did she know I was sending her to the University of Antarctica). It was probable that Luanne would marry her pedodontist once he recovered from his mourning for his daughter. I disliked cats. I would be alone more and more of the time.

Unless, of course, I picked up the telephone.

The following Wednesday I trailed Luanne across the beer garden to our favorite picnic table. Once we'd feathered our nest with beer, she handed me several typewritten pages.

"Wow," I murmured as I read the private investigator's report on Becca, who had too many aliases to list. "Hot checks, embezzlement, theft of property, check kiting, credit card fraud. She was accomplished, wasn't she?"

"A perfect con woman," Luanne said as she reached once more for a cigarette that wasn't there. "Her only flaws were greed and restlessness. She was married to wealthy old men. All she had to do was sit tight until one of them died and she could inherit a few million."

I continued to read. "Her last one died, all right. Becca didn't leave Miami because she was mugged—and her bruises came straight from her makeup kit. She left because the medical examiner found some exotic chemical in dear old Harry's blood."

"Dick might have found himself comparing notes with Harry," Luanne said. "If she hadn't decided to take the Dunling Foundation's money, she might have decided to be a black-clad widow."

"Does Captain Gannet have everything under control?" I asked as I put down the papers.

"He's stopped bothering Dick. There's no way to prove Becca was responsible for Jan's death, but Dick did remember that Becca had insisted Jillian take an antihistamine from one of her prescriptions. She also fixed him a nightcap at the party before they went home. As for Jillian . . ." She stopped and sighed, her face creasing with pain. "We won't ever know exactly what happened between her and Becca at the house. Becca's fingerprint was found on one of the computer keys—as, by the way, were many of yours. Dick is convinced Becca wrote the message after Jillian was unconscious."

"And the rest of the gang?"

"Gannet's staging daily press conferences regarding Agatha Anne and Georgiana's fraud and interference in an investigation. He met with the immigration officers last week, and the hawks and eagles will be applying their own Band-Aids in the future. The Dunlings have not been found yet, but Gannet's got a map on his wall and colored thumbtacks to mark their sightings. They're not as fashionable as Elvis. This may be the beginning of a whole new cult, however; Livia and Wharton are the new heroes of environmental groups across the nation."

"And the eagles?"

"They must have been piqued when nobody came to gape in wonder at them. They're gone."

We were both avoiding the obvious topic. I swallowed a mouthful of beer and said, "What about you and Dick?"

"I don't know. I haven't seen or spoken to him since the funeral. He left to stay at his mother's for a few days. He didn't know what he

would do after that. Sid called me this morning
to say that Dick had instructed him to put both
houses on the market."

"Did Sid say anything else?"

"He asked me out to dinner in some country
inn. I declined." She managed a shaky smile. "I
guess you were right, Claire. As loath as I am to
admit it, you usually are. You make up your mind,
and then stick to your decision."

I wondered if I ought to tell her about the upcoming Caribbean cruise.